HER ALIEN SAVIOR

ELLE THORNE

BARBED BORDERS PRESS

Thank you for reading!

To receive exclusive updates from Elle Thorne and to be the first to get your hands on the next release, please sign up for her mailing list.
Elle Thorne Newsletter

HER ALIEN SAVIOR

A sexy sci-fi new adult series starts with Her Alien Savior, a book that brings us Finn and Marissa. A sexy alien and the human hellion he can't resist, even when she's his intended target.

An alien soldier without emotions.

Finn is three quarters Asazi and one quarter human. He's a lieutenant in the Asazi army and his desire is to be the best soldier he can. He's spent a lifetime denying his human side, only to find out that now it makes him key to a mission on Earth. A mission that includes Marissa Sanchez, Target 41, a determined, smart-mouthed spitfire that brings out emotions his Asazi nature rejects.

A human woman with a target on her.

Marissa's dream is to keep her restaurant from being seized by ruthless developers. She's broke, out of options, has a deadline, and a cheating ex who offers to marry her and solve her financial problems. Everything changes when a guy named Finn saves her life and provides a completely different kind of option.

Elle Thorne Newsletter

If you can't click, just put this in your browser:

http://www.ellethorne.com/contact

CHAPTER 1

"Abort mission, abort mission." His commander's voice was clear through Finn's headset.

Curses. What is this about? "What is it, sir?" He kept his voice low.

"Your presence is required at the center."

Finn glanced around the dense, leafy foliage, down the path, and between the trees, but couldn't see any of his squadron. He adjusted his headset, pushed his helmet back off his forehead. This was unusual, interrupting a mission, even if it wasn't the real thing. It had to be something important. Maybe they'd been attacked. Maybe it was time for a real mission. Finn had been doing these practice missions for three weeks, and he was ready for some action—real action —again. Maybe there was an invasion. Maybe the

Kormic had penetrated an Asazi entry. He ran the back of his hand over his forehead. It came back streaked with camouflage paint, confirming his suspicion that he was a mess. And probably not a pleasant-smelling one. "Should I shower and clean up first, sir?"

"Negative. As is, soldier. As is. Report to the conference room at once."

Slinging his weapon over his shoulder, Finn double-timed back to the center, boots crunching the undergrowth. The entrance appeared suddenly in front of him, almost imperceptible unless one knew where to look. He shoved his ID into the recognition slot, and the door opened with a whoosh. Three heavily reinforced hallways and two ninety-degree right turns at dead ends later, he was standing in front of the conference room, almost out of breath. Not from exertion, but from anticipation. Hopefully this was good. A good assignment. A chance to infiltrate the enemy, take down some of them, sabotage one of their strongholds, maybe more than one.

He took a deep breath and knocked. *Curses.* He must be a sight, if the camo streaks on his hand were any indication. He didn't even want to know what he smelled like. He was a mess in front of his superiors, probably not a good thing. But surely they'd take into account that he was fresh from a mission. No, not fresh from a mission, interrupted and abruptly yanked from a mission. Worry about what they wanted coursed through him. A bead of perspiration made its way down his spine, between his wings.

"Enter." The voice was muffled behind the steel door that opened with a quiet whoosh.

Several men stood around the gleaming metal conference table, hands behind them, backs soldier-straight, chins tucked, but Finn's eye caught on one. His cousin, Kal.

He fought and defeated the urge to acknowledge his cousin in an unprofessional way. "Sirs." Finn addressed the room at large.

His commanding officer had a look on his face that made Finn nervous, but he couldn't figure out why.

No one said a word for more than a minute. All eyes were on him.

"Finneas Ramont, reporting as ordered, sir." Would that jar them from their silence?

"Soldier. Bad news. And an assignment. Which do you want first?"

What kind of choice was that? And what kind of bad news could they possibly deliver?

Finn unclenched his jaw. "News first."

Kal sported the same uniform Finn did, except his was pristine, not grimy, sweaty, or camo-streaked. It wasn't exactly identical because Kal's rank was higher than Finn's. Naturally so, since Kal was two years older than Finn.

Kal stepped forward. "Your grandmother. She passed."

Finn's breath was gone. His lungs felt empty. The last time he'd felt like this was when he was shot in the chest. Though he had body armor on, the impact was the same: breathlessness coupled with the most intense pain. He bit back the word *Nana*, his name for her. He wouldn't let them see the weakness, the emotions he held for her, the one who'd raised him. "My grandmother? How? When?"

"Age. She wasn't young. And we don't have the same medicines as humans. She is the only one of that kind here. Was the only one." His commanding officer corrected himself. "Last night. It was sudden. Unexpected."

Of course it was unexpected. Finn had been at her house ten days ago, before he left for the mission. She'd been all right. Smiling, laughing with him—her only grandchild. He swallowed a bitter knot of self-blame. He'd left her alone. He hadn't been there. No, he wouldn't have been there much anyway. Not when he'd spent so much time avoiding her when he was younger —denying his human side, even if he was only a quarter human.

He fought the sinking bereavement. He would deal with these emotions in private. Swallowing a knot of self-disgust and pain, coupled with self-blame, he asked, "The assignment, sir?"

"We are preparing for the Third Wave. We want you to go. Your experience, your instincts, your bloodline—they could all be valuable when we access Earth again, during the Third Wave. This Wave must succeed."

Finn grabbed the table's edge as he tried to absorb this assignment. The table's cool surface was smooth but not reassuring under his fingertips. "You want me to go to Earth." All the time he'd spent denying the human in him, all this time, repelling it. *And now this.*

Marissa stared at the envelope. Certified mail. Addressed to Marissa Sanchez. Owner of Two West Two.

Certified mail was never good news. What could it be now? She didn't want to open it. She shoved it on the dash. *Screw this.* It could wait until tomorrow.

She turned the key in the ignition. She had work to do. Lots and lots of work, since she was working with a skeleton staff at the restaurant now. Odd how there was this point in the restaurant business, in terms of volume and money-making, the point right before the restaurant became busy enough to hire the amount of help it would take to keep her from killing herself at work. Two West Two was not at that stage now. At one point, it had been, but that was some time back.

When she took a turn, the envelope slid across the

dash, reminding her that it was there, a reminder she didn't really need. It wasn't like she was going to forget what had to be bad news. Oh, shoot, she should have looked at the return address. That would have given her a clue. But now the envelope was all the way across the dash, unreachable. At least, not reachable in a safe way, not while she was in traffic.

It probably said IRS on it. That's what the last two certified letters had said.

No. she needed to know what it was. She pulled into a convenience store parking lot, parked the Honda, and reached across.

She turned the envelope.

The return address was her landlord's.

The man who owned the property that Two West Two sat on. She'd been leasing the land and building from him for years. And before Marissa, her father had leased it, when he owned Two West Two.

Why would Dan send her a certified letter? He had her phone number.

Fear raced its icy fingertips up her spine. This did not bode well. She took her cell phone out, hit speed dial for Dan.

Shouldn't she open the letter first? She pressed *END CALL* and ripped the letter open.

She scanned it. Got lost in the legalese. Then took a few moments to read it more thoroughly.

"Son of a bitch." Her voice wasn't much more than a

low whisper. She'd been on a month-to-month lease for a while now. She had never worried about renewing and Dan had never given her cause to think he was worried about it. She figured they had an understanding. He knew how much Two West Two meant to her. He wouldn't do anything to change that.

Wouldn't? that voice in her head asked. *He just did,* the voice reminded her.

Yeah, he sure did. He was selling the land her restaurant was on. Not all of it, but enough of it to mandate getting rid of the restaurant. Getting rid of her father's dream—her dream now.

She leaned back against the headrest. She wanted to call Dan and explode at him. Like that would do any good.

She could call her brother—no, no she couldn't.

She couldn't call the brother she hadn't spoken to in two years. The brother who had refused to come to their father's side while he was on his deathbed. Her brother had been too busy, couldn't handle it, had already said goodbye as far as he was concerned.

All of her brother's excuses amounted to one thing: Marissa had to be the only one there when their father died. She swallowed back the lump that always rose in her throat when she thought of the night Dad had passed.

The hell with it. She dialed her brother's number. A quick "Hello, how are you?" was the only formality she and her brother indulged in before he said, "What's up?"

"Dan's going to sell the land that Two West is on. I can't get the money to buy it out by myself. Thought you could help—"

"Marissa. I never cared about that stupid restaurant."

"But it was Dad's dream."

"He's dead."

Her brother's words sliced through the final bit of affection she harbored for him. "Yeah, I know. Sorry I asked. I'll figure it out."

And with a quick, "No problem," he hung up.

Just like that. What the hell had she been thinking, calling him?

Time to call the landlord. She pressed his speed dial number. He answered on the first ring.

"Dan. I got the letter." Shit, she should have said hi, how are you, something, anything. She surely wasn't acting like someone who wanted to ask him to let her have some time to come up with the money.

"I'm sorry, Marissa. I had an offer I couldn't turn down. Lizzy's sick, you know, and this would allow us —" His voice broke.

With his wife Lizzy sick, she shouldn't be surprised that the local developers were closing in like buzzards.

"Her medical bills, you know." Dan continued.

Marissa felt worse about calling the poor man. "I'm

sorry Dan. I understand." She didn't want to understand, but she did. He didn't need to be any more upset than he already was. "I'll see if I can make something work out with the bank to compete for the land purchase."

She didn't have that kind of money in her account. She had no money in her account. Yeah, she'd have to look into a loan.

"My lawyer, Joe Perry, he's handling it. He's a good guy. If you can make it work, somehow, he'll be there to deal with. But I have to say, if you can do it, I'll be happy for you. He's the reason for the certified mail, you know."

Marissa could almost picture Dan's characteristic shrug.

CHAPTER 3

"**I** think she would have liked her service."

Kal followed Finn from the mess hall. They walked the narrow path, reinforced against the enemies on the outside. They'd just left Nana's service, a simple funeral attended by few. Too few. Just two. And then a cremation. The luxury of burial in the ground didn't exist on this planet, not when space was limited by what area of land in Kormia they could protect from invasion.

Kal's father and Finn's father were brothers. They shared a grandfather who'd been married twice, first to Kal's grandmother, and then when she died, to Finn's grandmother. Even though Nana wasn't Kal's grandmother, Kal had been at her house more than any of their other cousins, so it would follow that Kal would attend the service.

It saddened Finn that there were only two of them in attendance. He and Kal, like always, closer than ever, than brothers.

"Yes, she would have liked her service very much." Finn felt the tension bunching the muscles in his shoulders. He didn't want to have the conversation that he was going to have with Kal, but he had to. "The mission..." He couldn't finish, didn't know what the consequences would be.

"What about it?" Kal turned to face him, brows drawn together.

Finn scrubbed at his face. He didn't know if his thoughts were from grief or if he was using this situation to gain the upper hand. Did it matter? He might as well forge onward. "I don't want to go. I'm thinking I'm going to pass on this assignment."

"It isn't exactly optional. It's not one of those. And it's crucial. How can you turn it down?"

"You say that when we just buried my Earth-born human grandmother? She was captured and brought over in the First Wave."

"And?"

"And I don't want to go to that planet. To see her people. To see the things she told me about." *To see the things I wish I could have.* He clenched his jaw at that thought. He had no business trying to have something or be associated with anything human. He'd fought all his life to not be human, to be more like his Asazi father. Curses be damned, he was confused.

"You're putting yourself above the Asazi. Our people need this. Our women are no longer able to conceive. Our species is going to die out. And it will happen before we make it to our Ultimate Passage. To reclaim our Earth. Our lands."

"Ultimate Passage is a myth. A myth that's kept alive by the old ones. I don't believe we had to make a passage here to this forsaken planet overrun by Kormic miscreants. A planet where we've had to spend every moment hiding or fighting off attacks. If we're from Earth, we should have returned long ago. We are superior to humans. Here we're sport and victims for the damned native creatures."

"It is not a myth. I believe the Sacred Writings."

Time for Finn to use some leverage. "Your father has power in the government."

"Naturally. He's one of the Governors-Select."

"I'll do the mission if you'll have him get me out of the Binding."

"Out of the Binding?" You want to nullify your Binding to Alithera?"

"I don't want to be Bound to her."

"She is fine marrying material. You've been Bound to her since you were two years old. The day she was born you were Bound to her. It was proclaimed. The ceremony is in a year, Finn. Your children will be born from those procured from the Third Wave."

"No."

"You haven't even heard what the mission entails. What you have to do. Surely you realize how much it matters. I choose to believe that this is your grief acting on you. You need a practitioner to check you out, to verify that you're sound physically as well as mentally. You don't seem well."

Days later, in his living quarters, Finn loosened his collar.

Kal leaned against the doorjamb. "Humans, especially the female of their species, are dangerous."

Finn ignored his cousin's cautionary words. It had been five days since his grandmother's passing and three days since he'd grudgingly accepted the mission. Very grudgingly, because he still didn't want this cursed assignment, even if he had been released from his Binding to Alithera, and even though the mission had been explained to him—in brief.

"When I joined the service, this wasn't what I planned to be doing. Posing as a human male to entice females." He unsnapped his weapon belt.

"You thought you'd always be wielding a weapon?

Killing?" Kal's skin fluoresced faint orange hues in ripples that traveled from his face to his arms, a sure sign he was becoming irate.

"I'm a soldier. So yes, something like that. Definitely not this." Kal's anger meant nothing to Finn, who concentrated on his pulse. That was the first step in conversion, to lower his heart rate to match a human's. It wasn't hard for him, not as hard as it was for others, because he was a quarter human, after all. He bit back the smirk that threatened to appear on his face. He would have to make sure not to let it rise, especially not rapidly, as his wings would burst through the human skin.

"Do you need the machine?" Kal reached for the equipment used to help them in their human conversion.

"No, I've got this."

"Well done, cousin. You're already sounding authentic." Kal didn't let the smile out, but Finn could see it in his eyes. Of course Kal wouldn't smile. That would be anti-Asazi. The Asazi prided themselves on being stoic and unemotional.

Finn snorted. Being converted into a human was definitely not how he'd planned to spend his military career. But like a good soldier, he did as directed. It was vital to the Asazi mission. Finn stretched in his newly acquired human skin, looking in the mirror.

"Not bad." Kal took a step back and studied Finn's reflection. "Not a bad specimen at all."

Finn's heart rate sped up. His chest expanded. He couldn't allow that to happen; it would convert him back to his native form. He bit back a growl of frustration. He was reverting. His skin glistened iridescent under the human layer of epidermis. His shoulders ached where his Asazi wings threatened to reemerge. He would be in so much trouble if he reverted while he was on Earth. Imagine if his wings erupted from beneath the human skin while people were around! Stupid wings. Why did the Asazi have them anymore, anyway? They were like appendixes in humans. Useless wings.

He'd asked his father about them when he was a child, why why the Asazi had wings they couldn't use.

"Once, long ago, we could use them. That was taken away from us," his father replied, but he wouldn't tell him who had taken flight away or why.

"Have you ever flown, Father?" he'd asked. "Or was it taken away before your time?"

His father had put his hand on Finn's shoulder. "I've never flown. It was long, long before my time, son. You know that already. The Sacred Writings say Asazi have not flown since the Banishment. It was part of our punishment."

"Finn, you cannot fail." Kal interrupted his reverie.

"You must not fail our people. Every targeted human female we can get is valuable—"

"And why are these women specifically crucial? Why can't we grab *any* women? Earth has an assortment of lesser populated areas where we don't risk discovery."

Kal's chin rose a notch, and he continued as if Finn hadn't posed a question. "And you are crucial to this mission. Please control the conversion." Kal took a step back, his eyes expressionless in the mirror.

Finn grit his teeth. "I'm trying, dammit." He didn't understand why they needed human women for this. "Why humans? Why can't we—"

"Much better. But I fear that your emotional outburst is not a result of your pretending. It's the human factor. You are part human, and that still wreaks havoc on your Asazi emotions." Clearly Kal didn't plan to address the second question.

Finn fought back his anger. No, he wasn't going to let that side of him win. He would control his emotions.

"The last thing you need is to convert in front of humans."

"I know. I get it. They'll capture me. Like they did the others."

"They killed Asazi with their experiments. I don't want that to happen to you, cousin."

"I know. I won't have a dissected body for you to

retrieve if I'm caught anyway. I'll make sure I'm dead and leave no trace of myself to be examined. So when am I to be dropped off? How many of us will be going?"

"You and nineteen others are slated for insertion tomorrow morning. Have you memorized your targets' files? All eighty of the targets are crucial. You have four, just like the others on your mission. Lucky you, you don't have to procreate with them. Don't lose your meal packs. Make sure you eat regularly. And do not eat human food. Ever. Your life depends on it."

Finn huffed his irritation with his cousin. "I'm not a child. I've been on countless missions. I know not to lose my meal packs. I know I have to consume sustenance at regular intervals."

"Fine. Fine." Kal had the decency to look embarrassed at his micromanagement.

"Cousin." Finn put a hand on Kal's shoulder. "Is it so bad? This procreation they indulge in?"

Kal looked away. "We don't want to be like them. They are an uncontrolled and uncontrollable race."

"But once, long ago, that was the method our people used to mate with humans. To produce... half-breeds." *Like me*, Finn wanted to add, but didn't.

"Like what happened with your mother," Kal continued. "Our methods have evolved. We are far more advanced than we used to be. We'll handle that once they're brought to the temporary station we will set up outside of Houston."

"What will happen to the women? What will be done with them? To them?" Finn's curiosity wouldn't let him rest.

"Enough." Kal's voice was gruff. "Do not reproduce with them, or indulge in copulation—sex, as they call it. It does strange things to human hormones. It makes them feel. It makes them do stupid things."

Finn didn't want to be on the receiving end of a lecture and he regretted asking. "Enough, already. Can we get going?"

"It makes them impatient."

Not funny. "Asshat." Finn frowned and took a mock-swing, at his cousin.

Kal ducked with an uncharacteristic laugh. "Very authentic human dialogue. Asshat? Really?"

Finn joined him in the laughter.

"Do not make mistakes." Kal turned serious. "I don't want to lose another family member to this cause."

"I won't." Finn became somber. Kal's oldest brother had been a part of the failed Second Wave of insertions. "So all I have to do is make sure they consume the formula. They'll be unconscious and I can deliver them to your team. That's it? But what happens to them?"

"We don't harm them. Unless... But even then, we are not the reason they come to harm. They have a reaction to the formulas and anti-serums. Don't concern yourself with that. You simply perform your role."

"But I didn't sign up for this. I signed up to be a soldier. Not to lure human females to our cause."

"They're called women. They're soft, sensuous, and occasionally... interesting."

Finn was pretty sure *interesting* wasn't the word Kal had originally planned to use. "You sound like you have experience with them."

"Only what I've heard."

Finn wasn't sure if he could believe his cousin, but it didn't matter at the moment. "I should talk to Alithera."

"You've been told not to. We'll handle telling her about the breaking of the Binding when you are gone."

"That seems evasive and underhanded. It's not my style. Let me tell her in person. Let me explain."

"Negative. Her father is a Governor-Select, as you well know."

"So? What does that matter?"

"She may press on him to delay the mission, to keep you here."

"She can't do that. Surely she wouldn't. Surely he wouldn't."

"We aren't willing to take a chance. These missions mean salvation for the Asazi."

"I don't agree with that method of handling her. She deserves better. Even if I don't—" Was he really going to say *Even if I don't love her? Since when did that come into play in Asazi Bindings?* Finn switched track immediately. "That doesn't change what I said. I didn't sign up to be a part of this. To be a part of your squadron. Anyway, isn't it against regulations to have relatives in the same squadron?"

"An exception was made. You're uniquely qualified."

"Because I'm a ruthless bastard."

"No one said that. Because you'll fight harder than anyone to keep emotions out of it."

Finn didn't want to hear that. It all boiled down to having a human female—a woman—as a grandmother.

"There aren't many left with the genetic composition you have." Kal clearly wanted to convince him, though Finn knew that the number was one, just him. But he'd put money on it that he'd been brought in because out of all the ones with human derivatives, he was the only one who was born of an actual human, and raised in proximity to a human. He knew humans personally. Well, one human—Nana. He had no siblings. And his grandmother had only had one child, his mother.

"Years of military training. Years of Elite Measures training. And what am I doing? I'm brought in to be an abductor. A kidnapper. Practically a seducer." He fought back a grunt of disgust. "Ridiculous."

"Ridiculous? How can you say that? Ridiculous to endeavor to propagate our species? To save Asazi? Your arrogance and belligerence is what I find ridiculous." Kal opened the door to Finn's quarters.

Finn snapped a salute.

"Not a seducer." Kal snapped one back.

Looking in the mirror, Finn studied his cousin's reflection, comparing it to his own—his new, human reflection. Not so very different. Not really, but yet in some ways, very different. The skin tone. The wings that Asazi folded, with barely a hint of protrusion. Never mind. Very different. If a human saw him in his natural form, he or she would think he was an otherworldly creature, but they wouldn't likely think he was from another planet. They'd assume he was an angel. Of course they would, what with the shimmering iridescent colors of his Asazi skin, and those wings.

They'd never believe this his people used to reside on Earth, long ago, before they were removed. Taken to another place, forced to learn new ways.

Finn lay on his bunk. His environment-controlled room suited his raging emotions. He knew that would change as soon as he arrived on Earth. Tumultuous, chaotic, disorderly Earth, populated with emotional, chaotic, tumultuous humans. Hunger seized him with a fierceness that reminded him it had been a while since he'd eaten.

He pressed a button on the headboard. Ten seconds and one swoosh, a meal appeared, perfect temperature, perfect nutrition. He held back a sigh, knowing that things weren't so simple on Earth, with its restaurants and fast food, processed foods. Asazi foods were processed, a part of him wanted to argue. Probably the human part.

He took a bite of the sustenance, which was devoid of flavor, but full of nutrients. What would his body do with different food? Kal had warned him not to eat any, but then again Finn had grown up with a human in his family.

No, he couldn't indulge that thought. He needed to do as he was ordered, not think about deviating. There was no point in thinking about human food. He wouldn't be indulging.

Thinking of human food brought his human grand-mother to his mind. During the First Wave, long ago, she'd been brought back and assimilated. She used to pull him aside and confide that he reminded her of her brother—a human. The day she had first told him that, Finn determined to never let his human side out. Being human was a weakness. Not that humans weren't likable; they were—but they were so damned flawed. So ruled by emotions.

From that day on, Finn strived for a perfected stoicism. And he avoided his grandmother.

He rolled over in his berth, disgusted, appetite gone. Damn it, he had never planned to be in the next move-ment to bring back humans. This was the Third Wave.

The Second Wave had failed, had left evidence on Earth that his kind had made it there. It had left the humans in a panic that they'd be invaded by Martians. He smirked at that thought. Martians, ha. The Asazi had waited decades to return, allowing the furor to die down, to turn into legends, whispers, conspiracy theories.

Studying human culture was not optional. The Asazi belonged on Earth, not these humans. One day, the Asazi would reclaim their place on Earth.

He wondered again what would happen to the women. What would be done to them? Would they live? Would they be kept captive? Would they be released? Or...

A small stab—emotional pain, human pain—caught Finn off-guard. He pushed it back. He didn't need to feel pain for his grandmother—a human. Kal's words invaded his mind: *It isn't bad to have emotions. Our kind do.*

What did Kal know? He had no human blood in him, no human ancestors. Kal's mother was 100% Asazi unlike Finn's mother, half-human, half-Asazi, who had died giving birth to Finn. It had been her choice, though she'd been warned not to, or so Finn's father had told him countless times. During childbirth, if the babies were not removed surgically, the human women died. But she was hardheaded, that half-human mother of his. His father would have a look of sadness on his face when he related that to Finn, sadness until his Asazi stoicism returned. Then it was replaced with nothingness, as if the sorrow had vanished. Or had never existed.

Finn's walk to the pod that would take the team from the carrier to Earth was like a prisoner's walk to the gallows. Each step was heavy. Why did it feel like he was walking to his own execution? Not that he had any experience with executions, or being a prisoner or a lawbreaker. No, not him. Not top-of-his-class Finn. He snorted in disgust, maybe even despair. And now he was here, the seducer of women. Snap out of it? Not that easy.

He slipped into his pod and strapped himself in. One of twenty, all of them lined up, ten on each side of the cabin. All converted to human males, and all soldiers. That gave Finn pause, but he didn't dwell on it for long.

He ran his hand over his human chest under the T-shirt. The sensation was oddly pleasing.

"Prepare to hibernate." The pilot's voice came through Finn's headset, warning him that sedative gases would be released in the individual capsules of those being transported for insertion. "You'll be uncon-scious until we're ready to insert you into the Earth population."

Finn wanted to ask if he could put himself back in his native body for the trip because of the energy it took to remain human. He knew better than to ask. He'd already been advised not to by Kal.

And he knew Kal was sitting next to the copilot. Kal was going with them. He would hear Finn's request, and Finn would hear about it later. And not in a good way.

CHAPTER 5

*M*arissa pushed her chair further away from the damned bank officer's desk, and hoped her heel scuffed the dark mahogany wood. She hoped it would leave a mark, but she didn't want to look. It so didn't matter right now, not after what he'd just told her. She fought to control her anger, but fury won out. "What do you mean, do I have someone to cosign? I've been in business for nine years. Why should I need a cosigner? My father had this restaurant for thirty years before he died—"

"Ms. Sanchez, times have changed. Have you looked at the numbers in the last few years?"

What she wanted to say was, *Why don't you fuck off?* But since he had no qualms about interrupting her, what she interrupted him to say was, "When two of the largest companies in the area relocate to different states, sales go down."

This was her fifth unproductive visit to the bank. Her fifth visit to this cold, impersonal, sterile environment. Why had she ever used to think that it was welcoming here? Things had changed. Funny how when you needed your bank, they crapped on you, but when they wanted your business, they were sugary-sweet.

"Do you have family who can cosign?" The bank's loan officer was back on that.

"No." Not really, anyway.

"Then—"

"Look, they're taking away a big part of my restaurant. Crooked developers." Yeah, she was pissed. All kinds of pissed. They were threatening her livelihood, the only thing she had left of her father's dream. No, dammit, she wasn't going to make it easy for them.

"This is progress, Ms. Sanchez. It's all in the name of progress."

"I can't afford progress."

"Surely you could get a job as a restaurant manager for one of the chains? One of the local restaurants that aren't floundering?"

He didn't get it. At all. This restaurant. Her dad. She fought tears of anger and helplessness. She wasn't going to give him the satisfaction of seeing her cry. Times like this, she wished she was the irrational, violent type. She'd love to pitch some Molotov cock-tails into the developers' homes... but she didn't even know who those faceless rich bastards were.

"Never mind."

She catapulted out of the chair. She had a restaurant to run and food to prep. And options to come up with.

MARISSA DICED THE ONIONS, telling herself that the tears that flowed were the result of the pungent smell while the knife she was wielding tapped out a machine-gun-rapid tempo on the cutting board. She had to figure something out. Damned developers.

Talk about a rock and a hard place. She wiped tears onto her sleeve, barely pausing with the chopping, as if she was taking her anger out on the onion. *Take that, county officials.* She stabbed the cutting board. *Take that, developers. Take that, stupid bank officer.* The onion was liquefying under the pressure of her knife.

A bell chime signaled that someone had come in the front door. A quick glance at the clock showed that it was way too early for business. Well, maybe not way early, but at least fifteen minutes before they were due to open. Earlier than she wanted to open, what with this grumpy mood of hers.

In the dining room, Belle's tinkling giggle was answered with a deep timbre. Male. And judging from

Belle's giggle, Marissa would guess attractive. Great. Just great.

Belle loved an opportunity to flirt. Not that Marissa blamed her. Sure, it'd be nice to have someone, but Marissa's luck with men wasn't all that great.

She should go check on the customer, whoever it was. *It's your restaurant, girl—every customer, every time.* Her dad's motto ran through her mind. That meant personalized service. She wondered if he'd still feel that way if he were here and faced losing the restaurant. All she wanted to do was sink into a hole, or crawl under a rock, anything as long as she could hide from the world and the failure she'd become.

Man up, Marissa. Put your big-girl pants on and get out there.

She put the knife down and rinsed her cheeks with a splash of cold water, then blotted with a paper towel. Marissa tried to plaster a smile on her lips, but her face hurt with the effort. Or maybe that was her heart.

She swung the stainless steel double doors open and stepped into the cool, inviting darkness of Two West Two's dining room. A man was leaning against the door, setting his backpack on a booth seat, talking to Belle.

Wait, did she say *man*? No, this was a hunk. All muscle, white tee that showed off strong pecs, dark hair, just long enough to run her fingers through, and a full set of lips with a ready smile.

Except that when he raised his eyes from Belle's enraptured countenance, gazing right into Marissa's eyes, Marissa would have sworn she saw recognition there. Not a glimmer of recognition; no, more like the kind of recognition a hunter gets in his eyes when he recognizes prey.

Surely she was mistaken. She had to be. Who would come in here seeking her out? Really, what man like that would be in here looking for her? She fought to keep a poker face, to keep from showing her confusion.

She didn't care for the way his glance made her feel. No, she didn't care for it one bit. Or did she? She rocked on the balls of her feet to keep from squirming under the intensity of his gaze.

The stranger took a step in her direction. Marissa stilled. Now what? What did he want? He wasn't dressed like a salesman, so probably not a restaurant supplier. He seemed more like—god, he looked more like the kind of man who would pose on the covers of romance novels.

The image of a bodice-ripper romance came to mind. No, not that kind. Marissa fought back a laugh, because he'd think her crazy for laughing out loud. The kind that he brought to mind was the sexy vampire stories, the ones with those beautiful men on them who'd make a woman wish she could meet a vampire. Yeah, that's what he looked like.

And good-looking men were bad news. Bad, bad

news. They attracted women. Lots of women. Women who had no qualms about sleeping with a man who was taken. Yeah, well, what about the men who did that? Way worse, Marissa agreed with herself. Not only did good-looking men do that, they also made women do stupid things. Yeah, no good-looking men for her. Give her an ugly dude any day.

He kept walking closer. Close enough for her to see the stubble on his chin and the deep, dark blue of his eyes.

"Marissa Sanchez?"

Marissa fought to keep defensiveness out of her voice. "Who wants to know?" And she lost. Defensiveness and outright hostility she couldn't control had come out.

Her vehemence clearly stunned him. He paused, then said, "I'm Finn."

"And that should mean something to me?" Oh god, why was she in such bitch-mode? Why? It could be because she was losing her restaurant. Her history. Her dad's dream. It was bad enough she'd lost Dad. "What can I do for you?" She made an attempt to soften her tone.

The man, Finn, turned back to Belle, probably wishing he could still be talking to her. Belle stared at him and defined the whole *batting eyelashes* phrase for Marissa.

And for some reason, for some damned reason that

Marissa didn't want to put her finger on, it pissed her off that he was wishing he could be talking to Belle instead. It made her wonder why she couldn't get past the feeling that he was looking for her, even though he wasn't exactly acting like it anymore.

CHAPTER 6

Finn took a look back at the nice one. Belle was her name, a plump one with pleasing curves and curly red hair, blue eyes. Of Irish descent, probably, if he'd studied his Earth history well enough. She stood near the entrance, holding a dark wood wall for support, as if she was going to swoon, giving him a look that said she would follow him anywhere, but preferably to a bed.

The lighting was dim, the décor simple, sconces casting the dark tabletops in a pale glow. Windows every few feet were half-shaded, keeping the heat and sunlight out.

He almost wished she were the one he was assigned to get close to. To bring back. Then he looked back at the girl referred to as Marissa in the paperwork. Marissa Sanchez. Target 41.

No, he'd keep this one, number 41, this Marissa. She wouldn't be easy to win over, that was clear, but there was something about her that appealed to him. Something fierce and passionate that made a reaction churn in his body, especially in the regions he'd been cautioned against using with humans.

He was confused. These strong sensations. This attraction... he hadn't felt that before.

She was a spirited little thing. She had a fire in those eyes, eyes the color of the lakes at home, not the ones on Earth—her eyes were green, almost iridescent—and she was dark-skinned, curvy. *Curses.* He fought the urge to focus on her body. Being human wasn't easy. He felt a stirring and worked his mind to rid his body of its impulses.

Were things more difficult for him because he was part human? Was that what made these things happen to his body? Or did all of the ones who were put on Earth go through this when they assumed human form? He'd have to remember to ask the others when they got back to the ship. Or should he? He'd probably sound stupid if he admitted to feeling things they didn't.

He kept his face stoic, something he'd practiced for years which shouldn't be hard to do, even in a human body, then looked into the little firebrand's eyes.

Why did she hate him already? Why such animosity toward someone she'd never met before? He took a guess. "Bad day? It's still early. I hope it hasn't been a bad day."

She fisted her hands, then unfisted them and put them behind her back. "No, just busy." She'd softened her tone, as if she'd realized how she sounded.

"Not a problem. I can come back later." He turned around and made for the door, wondering if she was going to call him back, or if she'd let him walk out. Surely she was curious. He didn't take long strides, hoping she'd relent, ask him what he wanted, why he was asking for her, that she would do something to stop him from going. He wanted to know more about this angry woman. She brought a whole rainbow of emotions to the forefront. He almost wanted to feign tripping and getting hurt to give himself an excuse to stay, but then he cursed himself. Impetuous emotions. He could always come back. She owned this establishment; it wasn't as if she was going anywhere.

As he passed her, Belle gave him a wink. He'd come back, alright. Under the guise of visiting Belle. She'd make things easier. He shot her a look and was rewarded with a blush that crept from her ample bosom to her cheeks. "I'll be back later for dessert."

Marissa. He'd come back for her. *It's business*, he told himself. *Strictly business. Sure*, the other side of him scoffed. *Sure it is.*

It has nothing to do with those eyes, that hair, that face, that body, that intensity, that anger, that passion. Nothing at all.

~

F INN LEFT THE COOL, dark, air-conditioned dining room of Two West Two and entered the already sweltering heat of Houston in July. Now what was up with that woman? Why the hostility? He couldn't fail this mission, his cousin, his people. Cursed humans. He wouldn't allow himself to fail something as simple as appropriating a human. He, who had been trained in Elite Measures, in the most difficult of military missions, would fail because of one ornery, pissed-off woman. He loved that term. Pissed off. His people needed a term as good as that one. How well that word fit sometimes.

The electronic cell phone Kal had provided him with chimed an alarm. Time to eat a meal. *Curses.* Double, no triple curses. Damn his idiocy. He'd been so caught up with the women... *Don't lie to yourself. You were caught up with that woman.* Truth be told, he'd been so caught up with Marissa he'd forgotten to pick up the backpack containing his food. It was still in her restaurant.

He didn't want to go back. Not now. Not like this. Did he? No. No way. But he had to eat. He had to sustain his body with food. Asazi food; Kal's words resonated in his mind. *Curses.*

But Finn was quarter-human. Surely he could survive on human food. Of course he could. His grandmother had made many meals for him. Countless meals, and nothing had happened. Why would this be any different?

Surely he would be all right. Yes, certainly he would.

The electronic cell phone dinged a signal that he had a communication waiting for him. His brother and the engineers had managed to secure a website that couldn't be found or traced to allow all of the Asazi on Earth to communicate with the ship that was harbored in North America, not too far from where they'd inserted Finn. Finn smiled; it was easy to say *not too far* when a vehicle traveled at the speed the Asazi ship did.

He had an email. Brief, and without a message that could compromise the mission.

Finn,

Tracking shows you are in place. All good? Need anything?

Kal

Damnation. Could Kal possibly know that he didn't have his food with him? Should he tell the truth? Confess? Would they send him more food? Or would they yank him from the assignment and label him incompetent?

For a moment he felt completely incompetent, then he shook it off. No, there was no way he would confess to this. In fact, he would deny it, if it ever came up.

Finn hit *Reply* and tapped a message in response.

All fine.

He didn't bother signing it, or addressing it to his cousin for that matter.

Okay, he wasn't fine, but he wasn't about to tell Kal about this spitfire, this woman, this Marissa. And he would never tell Kal about the food. Ever. No, there was no way he would let anyone know.

He used his electronic smart phone to find the phone number for the restaurant she owned, wondering why it was called Two West Two. He needed to get on her good side. How could he ever get her to the ship if he didn't? He had six days to get all the women to the ship before they departed for home. Six days. Four women. No, three women and this spit-fire. He hoped the other women would be easier to manage.

The image of her face came to mind. The set of her jaw. The hard determination in her eyes.

Six days.

He pressed the *Call* button next to the restaurant's phone number on the telephone's screen.

As it started to ring he realized he didn't have a plan. *Curses!* No plan, no thought of what to say. Should he mention the backpack? It would provide a good reason to return immediately. But was that what he really wanted? The damned thing stopped ringing. Someone had answered the phone.

Damn his impetuous nature. Damn his human blood.

"What a douche." Marissa couldn't help the phrase after she heard his comment to Belle. Here he was, asking for her, checking her out, and making a pass at Belle. Douche, for sure. Completely disinterested in interaction or conversation, she spun around, going back to her onions, tears, and thoughts. Except she wasn't that lucky. Belle followed her, the door swinging in and out on its hinges, in and out again after Belle released it.

"He's hot. Like, wow. Hot. Have you ever—"

"No," Marissa interrupted, trying to keep her tone even, but her foul mood was worsening after that encounter. She shouldn't take it out on Belle, though. "He's probably a cheater, just like every other..."

Marissa didn't feel the need to finish her sentence. It wouldn't have mattered anyway. The whole time she was griping, Belle was gushing. Normally Belle would stop to tell her that not all men were like her ex. That some men were good. But not today. Today she was too busy gushing.

Gushing about how hot this new guy was. Gushing about his pecs, his ass, his eyes, his arms, his face—everything. Marissa fought the impulse to tell her to stifle it.

In the dining room, the phone rang.

And again.

And again.

It didn't look like Belle was going to answer it.

Marissa wiped her hands on the towel, ran to the dining room and picked up the cordless phone. "Two West Two."

"Ms. Sanchez?"

Him. His voice. Finn. She recognized his voice.

She coughed. Then she couldn't stop. What the hell? What was wrong with her? And why was he calling her? She croaked out a "Yes?"

"I just wanted to apologize for upsetting you this morning. Not my intent, at all."

Why would he call her to apologize? Why not simply tell her when he came back to get dessert, as he'd told Belle he was going to do?

Maybe he didn't want Belle to know he was talking to her? Player. Cheater. Douche. Marissa dismissed him from her mind. "You're fine." Okay, not the thing she'd meant to say, not the way it could be interpreted. "What I meant was, it's fine. No problem."

There was silence on the phone. He either wasn't speaking, or he'd hung up, or they'd been disconnected.

Either way, she shrugged, and hung up the phone.

Marissa tripped over a backpack on the floor in front of the counter. She picked it up, then dropped it behind the counter next to the cash register and headed back to the kitchen.

"I kind of like him." Belle was droning on—still, as if Marissa hadn't just left the room.

As if the ass hadn't just called Marissa and tried to talk to her. As if he hadn't just tried to sweet-talk her.

As if.

Marissa fought to keep the bitterness she felt at his duplicity from showing. She forced a smile to her face. "I couldn't tell." Marissa tried to widen the smile, to make it reach her eyes, to keep from snapping what she wanted to say, which was something along the lines of, *I'm losing my restaurant. I'm losing everything. And you're drooling over some guy? A douche of a guy, actually. Really?*

Okay, she needed an attitude adjustment. She really did. It wasn't Belle's fault. It really wasn't that guy's fault, either. And Marissa seemed to be affected by him as much as Belle was. Okay, maybe not as much, but a whole lot more than she wanted to be. She shoved the onions into the reach-in, threw the cutting board in the sink, and made her way back to the dining room.

If he showed up to have dessert with Belle, she'd buy his dessert and let Belle sit down and visit with him. They could call it a date. She'd surprise Belle with that nice gesture when he came.

Ugh. She tried to quell a spark of jealousy.

If, the voice of doubt said. *If he shows, because you know that men don't follow through.* But Dad always did, she argued with the voice. The one that said everything she never wanted to hear. She hated that voice.

CHAPTER 8

She'd hung up on him. She did. It shouldn't matter. But yet...

Hunger roared in Finn's stomach, demanding satisfaction. He ignored it and went back to the hotel room, where at least the temperature would be tolerable compared to the Houston heat and humidity.

He stripped off his human clothing and lay on the cool bedspread, allowing his Asazi form to return. He closed his eyes, but the images of the dark-haired, green-eyed spitfire wouldn't go away.

Finn reached for the remote, turned on the television and tried to immerse himself in the interests of humans.

He could not. The programming held little of interest, and Marissa would not stop plaguing his mind. He had time to kill before returning to Two West Two.

Spying the files, he tossed the remote on the bed and sat up. When he flipped the top one open, he found himself looking at that green-eyed vision's driver's license photo. Marissa Secilia Sanchez. Target 41. Suddenly, knowing what would happen to the women mattered. He never paid attention to rumors or whispers, especially ones that didn't concern or involve him, but he'd heard stories about what had happened to human women in the First Wave. His grandmother was an exception, because the Asazi in charge hadn't counted on his grandfather falling for a human. His grandfather hadn't even counted on that.

That had changed a few things. First, she was taken out of the isolation that the human women of the First Wave had been put into. She was brought to live with the Asazi, to assimilate. She did a good job, but no other human woman was allowed to do that. She wouldn't have been, either, except Finn's grandfather was a top-ranking general in the army. The others weren't about to tell him no.

Finn had heard that things were different now, that Asazi technology had improved, that the dangers and methodology had changed. *Live female humans are no longer needed. There is no reason to accommodate transporting them.*

What in the curses' name did that mean? If not live females, then—

A brief image of Marissa—pale, eyes clouded over in death—crossed his mind.

He didn't want to think of that. He looked at the cell phone, wanting to call Kal, to ask for details. He punched the headboard, trying to jar the visual away.

He fought the urge to call Kal, his Asazi sensibilities battling with his human urges, his military training fighting his emotions. He couldn't call Kal. That would create complications, draw attention to his human qualities, his ability to remain objective. These types of assessments of him would derail his military career. They'd lose respect for him and he'd be lost behind a desk, forever. No assignments, no missions, no excitement, no promotions. Just a dull, dreary, cubicle-centered life.

Then what were his options? He paced the room, picked up the remote again, flipped channels mindlessly.

His image in the mirror caught his eye, actually catching him off-guard. Not because he was in his Asazi form, but because his usual shimmering green hue had been replaced with orange undertones. Green represented calm. These orange undertones were becoming more pronounced with every second.

Orange. The color of anger. A color and an emotion that rarely made its appearance in Finn. He'd always worked hard to control his emotions. And he'd always succeeded. He prided himself on that success.

Evidently he wasn't succeeding this time. He didn't want to see his angry orange Asazi color. He'd sooner take on his human form. He muttered a curse, controlled his pulse, manipulating it, beginning the conversion to human once more. His wings folded, receded. His skin became a ruddy human color once more.

He flicked the remote. One channel. The next channel. Another one. And another one. And another.

Loud moans stopped his rapid procession through the channels. A woman was on the screen, one with long dark hair, nude, sitting astride a man, rocking herself on his body. Her head was thrown back, hands cupping, caressing her breasts.

A strange sensation, an unfamiliar one, not unpleasant, tugged at Finn's groin area. A glance confirmed what he hadn't yet experienced in his human body. His male member was standing at near-bursting attention. He wrapped a hand around his thickness and was rewarded with a jolt of pleasure.

On the screen the woman dismounted, pushing herself off the man, revealing his own thick, swollen member, glistening with her juices. She leaned over him, and the camera closed in on her face as she lowered her lips and took him in her mouth. A moan erupted from the man.

Finn stroked his erection in the same rhythm that the woman on the screen lowered and raised her head, seemingly swallowing the man's erection in its entirety. A shudder coursed through Finn's body and a drop of liquid seeped out from the slit on his pulsing, mushroom-shaped head.

The camera panned away from her face and circled around her body, momentarily focusing on breasts that swayed with every motion as she bobbed her head and swallowed the man's thickness.

Then the view changed, completing a trip around her body, finally closing in on her sex. Mesmerized, Finn stared at her swollen, dripping center. He stopped stroking, transfixed. As if sensing his need to see more, she spread her legs, revealing a dark pink interior that pulsed and flexed, as if it was playing a peek-a-boo game he couldn't tear his gaze from.

He hadn't noticed when he resumed stroking his shaft, fingers firmly wrapped around that swollen part of his body. But he was very aware now that he was doing it, and the faster his hand moved, the shallower his breathing became.

The effect was natural, yet foreign. Asazi didn't practice these base human actions even though they had the same body parts.

With the Asazi, offspring were designed and planted in order to create better beings, whereas humans left these things to chance and emotions labeled as lust or love. And look where that got them. Nowhere, as far as the Asazi were concerned.

A part of his brain forced his hand to still, but he couldn't contain it for long. He started again. He couldn't refrain from the strokes that brought the intense pleasure.

Had it not been for human emotions, be they lust or love, his Asazi grandfather would not have claimed his human grandmother or created his half-human mother.

He pushed those thoughts aside.

A sensation of flying through a vortex seized him. The woman on the screen was remounting the man's shaft, lowering herself onto him in a smooth, gliding motion, piercing her inner core with his shaft.

Her full posterior was inviting. Finn's hand moved faster, gripped tighter. The vortex intensified. For reasons he couldn't understand, green eyes and a set of full breasts crossed his mind. And stayed. Marissa. Target 41.

The vortex spun out of control. Finn ejaculated, filling his hand and exploding onto the dresser.

He sat on the bed, exhausted, drained, confused.

Sleep came easily, but it was short-lived. He awoke to a hotel room that was fully lit and a TV emitting the white noise of static.

Still confused, he knew one thing. Until he was certain of what was in store for Marissa Sanchez, 41, he wasn't turning her over to his cousin.

He picked up the cell phone and typed an email message to Kal.

Rearranging order. Target 41 out of town. Proceeding to 42.

Finn pressed send and picked up 42's file.

CHAPTER 9

It was almost midnight. Two West Two was quiet; everyone was gone. It hadn't been a busy night, but Marissa was tired. And she was in a bad mood, a hell of a bad mood. If she'd have cared to admit it to herself, part of it was probably attributable to that man. That... She searched for a better word than 'man', but couldn't bring herself to call him a douche again, even in her own mind, especially since he stirred up a whole mess of feelings inside her. Conflicted feelings. Confusing ones, too, since she didn't get where they came from or why they existed.

It had to be a combination of stress, fatigue, and shock from all this crap. What else could it be?

The guy called Finn hadn't come back to the restaurant. He hadn't come for dessert with Belle. Nor did he come for the backpack that Belle said belonged to him.

Marissa glanced at the black and gray backpack. She wanted to know what was in it. Yes, she was curious about this man.

But she shouldn't. No, she shouldn't. She put her hand on the zipper. *You know better than to open other people's stuff, even if you're curious.* She yanked her hand back.

But what if it held some information that would help her get it back to him? Should she look in there to find it? *You know better. You just want to pry, maybe even see him again.*

She didn't want to admit to that, so she turned away from the backpack. He'd come back for it if it was important.

But what if it contained medicine that he needed? Like, if he was a diabetic or had heart issues?

A body like that? Her inner voice scoffed. *As if that body would need medicines.* His image flashed through her mind. That was a fact.

She reached for the light switch, banishing Finn's body and face from her mind. A good night's rest would give her a fresh perspective.

And maybe give you some answers to your problem.

That was true. She had no more clue what to do about the restaurant than she'd had this morning when that jackass at the bank had jerked the rug out from under her feet.

What could she do, though? Nothing. She scrubbed

at her face with hands that hurt from chopping vegetables and carrying large entrée plates all day. Yep, there was nothing she could do.

Or was there? Surely she could do something about it? Couldn't she? If she had the money to buy the chunk of property the landlord was selling, the chunk that included Two West Two. Wouldn't that solve the problem?

Maybe, maybe not. There was still the issue with the declining business. *Yeah, but what if I offered catering? Hired a catering manager?*

Sure, with what money?

That again. It all boiled down to money, didn't it?

The door chimed.

What the hell. James hadn't locked the front door when he left. Marissa froze. Taking a deep breath, she reached for the bat by the register. *Like that'll help if the intruder has a gun.*

"Marissa?"

That voice. She knew that voice. Joey. Her ex. She released her grip on the bat, her fingers still stiff from fear. "Yeah." Her voice betrayed her anxiety. She hoped he wouldn't notice.

"Why is the door unlocked? You need to talk to James about that."

"I know. What do you want?" She couldn't keep the civility from draining from her tone. She had no reason to be nice to him.

"Nice to see you, too." Sarcasm colored his voice. He raised his hand, holding a bottle of wine. "Your favorite." He was still hot. Corporate hot. Conservative hot. Not dangerous hot.

And just like that, her mind flew to Finn. Dangerous, hot Finn. "I hate wine."

He tilted his head, the sexy way that used to drive her crazy. "Since when? You loved it when we were together. You drank it every time I bought it."

That head tilt might have driven her crazy, but she remembered the shit she'd put up with from him. "You never asked. It's all you bought. I indulged you."

He put his hand over his heart, as if he was wounded, mortally wounded. "Ouch. Way to make me feel like a heel." But there was still a twinkle in his eye.

Marissa was ready for him to be gone. "Why? Because you cheated on me?"

He recoiled, as if he was shocked she'd bring it up, or remember, or hold it against him. As if. "Does that keep us from being friends?"

"I'm not sure we ever were friends. Friends don't rip their friend's heart out over a piece of ass he met at the gym."

Joey nodded. Acknowledging her point, probably not conceding it, if she knew him. "Just one drink. Come on. I know you're having a rough time."

Marissa pushed the tip jar to the corner of the counter. She'd let Belle handle that later.

Wait. Wait. What? What did he mean? "Exactly what kind of rough time is it you think I'm having?" She yanked the scrunchie out of her hair, releasing the curls, and scrubbed the tension away with her fingertips, all that without taking her eyes off Joey. Waiting, waiting for an answer to her question.

His Adam's apple did a bob. She knew that bob oh-so-well. Joey was working on an answer.

She tapped on the cupboard, studied her nails. Damn, they looked bad. She missed the days of French manicures, of pampering. Yeah, well, that was a long time ago.

"Well?" she prodded Joey.

"I went to school with Rudy."

Rudy. The a-hole at the bank. The one whose desk she'd hoped she'd scuffed.

"Your friend sucks."

"It's not exactly in his control, you know."

"Why the hell is he discussing my private business with someone it doesn't concern?"

"Wow, Marissa. You're not retracting your claws in the least today." He took a few paces in her direction, then detoured to the server station, where he picked out a corkscrew and two wine glasses. "It's not a conspiracy or anything like that. Anyway, I thought maybe I could help."

"Really? Like, what kind of help?" She didn't trust him in the least. If Joey's mouth was moving, he was lying. "You're in car sales. What are you gonna do? Give me a job selling cars?"

He turned the corkscrew into the cork. Twisted it out and set it down. "Well, yeah, I guess, if that's what you want. But I was thinking of something else. Something to help you keep Two West Two."

He had her attention now, though she still wasn't ready to buy whatever he was selling. "Keep talking."

"I could give you the money, and you could make me a partner."

Marissa opened her mouth to tell him there was no way in hell she'd sign any part of her father's business over to him.

He raised his hand, stopping her before she'd even begun her protest. "There's another option. Hear me out."

She waved her hand like a cop controlling traffic, leading him forward. "Go on."

"Marry me."

"What?" She couldn't have heard him correctly. Couldn't have. There was no way. "Marry you? Why the hell would I want to do that? Why the hell would you?"

He took a sip of the wine he'd poured, then sauntered to the counter, still the same old cocky Joey, and handed her a glass. "Why don't you just think about it before you give me an answer?"

Marissa set the glass down. She wasn't even

remotely interested in drinking wine. She hated wine. It gave her a headache. And right about now, Joey was giving her one too.

His option wasn't quite the option he thought it was. It wasn't the option that anyone who didn't know Joey would think it was.

She closed her eyes and rubbed her temples. Shuffling sounds made her hope that Joey was leaving. Without stopping or even opening her eyes, she said, "Lock the door, please."

Taking a short nap on the cot in the back sounded good right about now.

A hand on her shoulder made her jump. She'd thought he was leaving, not walking her way. The hand resting on her other shoulder wasn't quite the same shock, but when the hands started to travel down the sides of her body, cupping the sides of her breasts before drifting to her hips, she had to put the brakes on.

"Joey, I can't even think straight. Give me some time."

"Think about my offer." His voice was soft in her ear. The same voice that used to make her body react to his touch.

He brushed his lips over hers.

She didn't open her eyes until she heard the door latch and click.

CHAPTER 10

Target 42 was a dog groomer in southeast Houston. Reluctant to check out of the hotel that was near Marissa, Finn thought over his choices.

Don't, he told himself. *Don't leave her behind.*

I won't. He wouldn't leave her.

The procedure to bring the targets in was simple enough, once initial contact had been made. An additive to a beverage would make the targets complacent and agreeable. Then twenty minutes later they'd be unconscious. And they'd better be in a secluded place or there would be questions asked, suspicions raised if anyone was around. Kal recommended a vehicle, for easy transport.

"Sounds simple enough," Finn mused. Much

simpler than many of the training missions he'd been on. He'd succeeded at those, succeeded very well.

The phone buzzed. Finn checked Kal's response.

Are you on schedule?

Finn paused. Should he tell Kal he might be behind? No, absolutely not. Better to try to catch up. He'd lost half a day. Or more.

His response to Kal was short. *Yes.*

After grabbing a kit that contained the necessities for securing the target, Finn set out for his rental and the forty-nine minute drive to southeast Houston.

FINN NOSED the rental into the parking lot of 42's apartment complex, riding the brakes to keep from going too fast, and easily identified her car.

Based on research, 42 shouldn't be coming out of her apartment until 7 a.m., at which point she'd go to her favorite coffee shop and order her usual.

42. He didn't want to remember her name. That would mean getting personal. What if the same thing happened with her as had happened with Marissa?

No... He knew the same thing wouldn't happen. *Not the same, exact thing,* but what if he started to care? What if his mission was impeded? No. That couldn't be allowed to happen. He would lose everything. He'd be a disgrace. Maybe he'd be court-martialed for treason. And he wouldn't blame them.

No. No friendships, no bonds, nothing. Just efficiency. Just transporting the target to Kal's team. That was all.

An apartment door opened. 42's door. He verified that this was the woman in the file photo, then followed her to the coffee shop. He parked and vaulted out of the car, dashed inside and ordered her favorite drink before she even opened her own car door.

Then he proceeded to the sugar-and-cream counter to doctor the coffee and wait for 42. *Teresa,* he reminded himself. *Teresa. You can't go around calling her 42.*

"Teresa." The barista called her name and handed 42 her latte.

42 approached him, her face distracted, deep in thought, maybe. Finn ran into her, jarring her elbow, sending her drink flying. Her expression turned to one of horror as coffee splattered him, the tables, and the floor.

"Jesus, I'm sorry," he apologized, reaching for napkins, doing his best to appear contrite. "I wasn't paying attention. Let me buy you another. What did you have?"

"A latte."

"Oh, hell, take mine. That's what I drink."

"I couldn't possibly." Her pale cheeks blushed a rosy color. She clearly wasn't immune to male attention.

"I haven't had a single sip yet. Not one." Finn pressed the drink into her hand. "It's yours. Take it. Can I get you a pastry? I feel bad. I wasn't paying attention to where I was going. Do you have time for a quick bite?"

He knew she had the time. Her usual routine included drinking her coffee at a park while she read a paperback romance.

"Oh, I—" She blushed a deeper red. "Okay. Why not."

"Want to sit outside?"

Twenty minutes later she was getting into Finn's rental, not only willing but also smiling, thanks to the Asazi supplement in her coffee.

In the car, she turned doe eyes his way.

Finn avoided looking into her eyes. He started the car, reaching for the stick to shift it as 42 sighed and laid her head down. Just like that, she was out.

Damn the curses, that was close. One minute earlier and she'd have passed out in the coffee shop. Exactly what he did *not* need. He wiped the sweat from his brow with the back of his hand. Between the humidity and heat in this city and the stress of making sure she was in the car before she passed out, he'd gotten drenched in no time.

Now for the drive to Kal and his group, who had set

up a compound northwest of Houston, not far from College Station.

The drive to the compound lasted more than an hour, a long drive during which all he could do was hope that the target wouldn't awaken. He had never asked how long the targets would be kept unconscious by the formula. If she woke up, he would have to come up with a plan instantly, and he would risk discovery. Not knowing these facts, as small as they may have seemed, made Finn nervous.

He nosed the car up to the hill that housed the compound they'd set up for the procedures to be conducted on the women, lifted 42 out and carried her to the tunnel that was well disguised by a thicket of shrubbery.

Another car pulled up. A different soldier, Merck, carrying another unconscious woman.

Finn nodded to him. "Your first?"

Merck frowned, then looked at 42. "No. My second. This one is your first?"

Finn didn't want to answer. He didn't need the attention, but now it was out. And here he'd thought he wasn't doing too badly. "Yes, my first was out of town."

"Perhaps our Reconnaissance and Surveillance Team isn't quite up to par. You should write it up."

Sure. And get caught lying. "Good idea." The words slipped off his tongue way too easily.

Two scientists accompanied by a trio of soldiers

came out to greet them. One of the soldiers was Kal. He had a suspicious look in his eyes.

"Take the subject." Kal pointed to 42.

When Finn was relieved of his burden, Kal put a hand on his shoulder. "A moment, cousin?"

Curses on the shadow of fire. He didn't want to stay for a talk. The others slipped through the opening and shut the compound off, and Kal started to walk away from the entrance. "Follow me, please."

As soon as they were a few paces away, Kal stopped. "I'm concerned." That was mild. That meant Kal was worried. Extremely worried.

"Don't be. Everything is well. I'll be on track before the third subject is due."

"I'm wondering if this was a good idea. Putting you on this assignment."

"Why?"

"I wondered what it would do to you. I know you went through a lot with Nana."

Finn drew his shoulders up, stood straighter. "People die. Asazi die. It's part of the cycle of life."

"I wasn't simply referring to her death. I'm actually thinking of your whole life. Of all the struggles you've had."

"What do you know about my struggles?" Finn fought to keep from reverting to his Asazi form as strongly as he fought the urge to strike at Kal.

"You've been closer to me than my own brothers. I've seen you. Watched you go through levels of hell."

"I don't need you in my head, and I don't need a practitioner, not for my body and definitely not for my mind. And you are not studied in the art of practitioning."

"I'll say no more." Kal turned toward the hilly entrance. "No. I'll say one more thing. I'm willing to support you in any decision you make."

What that meant, Finn wasn't sure. He also wasn't sure why Kal felt the need to say it. "Thank you."

Kal stepped toward him, put his hands on Finn's shoulders, and looked him in the eyes. "Any. I mean it. Anything you choose to do, any decision. I'm here for you."

Finn didn't know why Kal had said what he said. He didn't know what extreme Kal was willing to go to when he made a proclamation of that sort, but he knew that if Kal made a decision that was rash and extreme, it could cost him dearly. "Why would you do that?"

Kal turned and walked away. Finn didn't allow him to go more than a few paces before he called his name. "Kal, I have a few questions for you."

"I assumed you would. And you know that there's danger in the questions you'll pose."

"Questions don't create danger. Actions do," he argued, but he knew he was lying to himself. The thing was, he was certain Kal knew too, from the look in his eyes.

"Ask them. But then I'll ask you one question in return."

"The women. Nothing happens to them? We don't kill them?"

"We don't kill them. But there are always things that happen in medical procedures, even when the utmost care is taken."

"And what will happen to 42?"

"She'll be home in four hours."

Finn nodded, but wasn't completely convinced, though he didn't know why. He didn't think Kal was lying to him, but something made him wonder, gave him pause. It concerned him.

"My turn." Kal rubbed his jaw. "41—she wasn't out of town, was she?"

Finn wanted to lie. He truly did. But he had never lied to Kal. They'd always been too close. "Not exactly."

Kal turned on one heel and marched back toward the entrance. "Go get your next target," he said over his shoulder. "If you need anything, let me know."

FINN DROVE BACK to Houston with Kal's questions and assurances heavy on his mind. He took the rental car to a parking spot at a truck stop and studied the files for

43. Downtown Houston. He drove the distance and parked outside her gym, then he waited. For five hours he waited, but there was no sign of her. She should have arrived four hours ago.

He drove by her apartment. Her car was nowhere in sight. Her job, the same, no sign of her.

Should he contact the team and tell them she wasn't around? After telling them that Marissa was gone? Kal knew the truth about that, but Finn was sure Kal wouldn't tell, even if his life depended on it. But after saying Marissa was out of town, Finn didn't think it would look good for him to have another missed target. Maybe he should move on to 44.

He planned to move on to 44, but for some reason, some cursed reason, he drove to 42's apartment. It had been more than four hours. It had been seven. No. Eight.

Her car wasn't in her parking spot. The lights were off in her apartment. This could be nothing. Probably was. But he wanted to be sure.

He parked down the street and decided to walk by her place.

He wasn't even halfway down the block toward her apartment complex when he walked by an appliance store with televisions in the window. Televisions with 42's picture on them.

Finn stopped. He tried to hear the news story through the glass, but couldn't. He didn't really need to, though. He could see what the story was about when her picture flashed onscreen again and above it was the word MISSING.

Kal wouldn't have lied. Finn believed that with all he held to be true. But something had happened. And until he knew what—

He tapped out a message to Kal on his phone.

What happened to 42?

Two minutes later, a reply came from Kal.

What do you mean? The Installment team returned her hours ago.

CHAPTER 11

Marissa picked up a package of chewing tobacco from the corner store. Her father had never liked flowers. He thought they were a waste of money, and he had never seen the point of putting flowers on graves. So she wasn't going to take him flowers. She put the chewing tobacco in the same bag that held the fishing lures she'd taken out of Dad's tackle box. She'd taken a moment to use a pair of snips to clip the hooks off. Couldn't have a stupid bird or squirrel seeing the lures and deciding they were lunch, only to be hooked. Now the lures were rendered useless, at least at hooking.

Along with the tobacco, the lures seemed like the perfect thing to put on Dad's gravesite.

The drive was long, because he'd asked to be buried near the coast he liked to fish so much. So she'd found the cemetery closest to his fishing spot, off the jetties in Port O'Connor and had gotten him a plot there. It was the best she could do at the time. Little did she know it would have cotton fields right next to it. Dad had loved cotton fields, had said they reminded him of his childhood.

She parked her car and jumped out. The sky looked like rain on the horizon, across the cotton fields and pastures. It smelled like rain, too. Just what she needed, to be caught in a summer thunderstorm on the Texas Gulf Coast.

What she needed was time to talk to Dad about what she was going through, about what she was thinking. She put the tributes beside his headstone and traced his name with her finger, the stone rough and yet warm against her fingertips. Just like Dad. Rough on the outside, but always warm.

She sat by the stone—no way could she sit on the gravesite. That seemed just... wrong.

"Dad." She bit her lip, unsure where to start. "So, Dad, it's not looking so good at Two West Two. I don't think I can keep the restaurant much longer."

Marissa picked at a blade of grass, folding its symmetry in half lengthwise. "I know you said I should pursue my dreams. I guess that makes me a loser. I thought I was. I thought pursuing your dream would be mine."

She hugged her knees to her body. "I know you said

not to. You said to do what made me happy. But I don't know what the hell that is. I wish I did. I wish I knew what I was meant to do."

A rustle came from behind her.

Marissa jumped up, not sure whether she should fight or flee.

"Marissa?"

"Joey. What the hell. You could have given me a heart attack." She put her hand over her chest. Her heart was beating faster than her pet rabbit's had the day a dog had chased it. Marissa had held it in her hands, trying to comfort it while the rabbit's heartbeat raced against her palm. "What the—what are you doing here?"

"I came to talk to you."

"You followed me?" She would have been nervous, but Joey wasn't the kind who ever made her doubt her safety when he was around.

He had the decency to look sheepish, and cast his eyes away. "I guess."

"Why?" Hostility cast an abruptness on the word.

"I wanted to tell you that I meant it. That I meant every word I said last night. Have you given my options any thought?"

"Yes. And I've given a lot of other things a thought. You were right. We don't belong together. Not even to save Two West Two."

"Wait a minute." His expression was caring. His golf

shirt was immaculate, and his khaki pants perfectly creased. Nothing was out of place. "I never said that. Never said it at all."

Everything about him was perfect. And at the same time perfectly fake.

"You didn't have to *say* it. You showed it when you cheated on me. You didn't even have the integrity to break up with me before you slept with someone else. And then you thought you'd keep it from me."

"How long are you going to punish me for that? To keep us apart?"

"Is that what you think I'm doing? I'm not apart from you because I'm punishing you. I'm apart from you because—" She took a deep breath. "We. Are. Not. Together. That's it. Period."

He opened his mouth.

She intercepted his statement, protest, whatever it was going to be. "Just go. Please. I'm trying to visit with my father. To sort out my thoughts."

"I just hope you make one of the things that you're sorting out my proposal. I want you to give it some serious thought. I'm in a position to help you."

A sigh was pushed out of her body, almost as if it wasn't her own doing. It flowed along with the words that came out. "I know, Joey."

CHAPTER 12

Finn didn't know how to reply to Kal's email that the Installment team had returned Number 42. Anything he said would confirm that he wasn't doing what he was supposed to be doing. That he was going maverick on them.

Another message came in from Kal.

Why do you ask that? Are you compromising the mission? Are you compromised?

He wasn't going to reply.

He only had one choice: return to the hillside and see what the Installment team really did with the human women when they were done with them.

He drove to their temporary Earth compound under the hill, went past it a short distance and parked the car behind a barrier of mesquite trees. Then he worked his way back toward the compound, roaming through pastures and fields, avoiding the highways and unpaved country roads.

His phone buzzed in his pocket.

Another email. Kal again.

The commander wants you to come in. Someone else will finish your job.

Too late. He was already in, but he wasn't about to tell them that. And there was no way in the Sacred Writings he'd ever allow anyone else to take over his mission. They'd bring Marissa in. Not a chance he'd let that happen.

He turned the phone completely off without responding and took up a spot behind a tree. He focused on the entrance, waiting to see what would happen when the Installment team came out. He'd follow them all the way in to Houston to see if they dropped off a live woman or if he'd been lied to.

Finn didn't have to wait long to see the Installment team come out carrying a woman. They paused outside the entrance and had a short conversation. But it was long enough for Finn to see one thing: she was breathing. Her chest rose and fell with each breath.

Relief flooded through his body. Kal had not lied... but that didn't explain what had happened with 42. It did tell him that his people weren't killing the human women. He could go back to the woman now. To Marissa. To 41.

The lunch rush was a bitch that day—the good kind of bitch. If only every day was like this, Marissa thought as she pushed in the till drawer on the register. If only. But she knew better. This used to be the trend, but not lately. Now it was the exception. And since it was an exception, that meant she didn't staff her restaurant accordingly, which meant she busted her ass waiting tables, washing dishes here and there, and bussing most of the plates.

As she passed the mirror on the wall in the smaller dining room she caught a glimpse of herself. *Holy buckets*. Oily sheen on her face, no lipstick left over, even her blush had sweated off. No point in making repairs now. It was two in the afternoon. Not likely they'd have any visitors. Not many, anyway. An occasional late straggler and then the early-birders around four to four-thirty.

Oh, well. As soon as she finished bussing these last few tables and put away some dishes, she'd cut the staff down to bare bones—meaning just her and Belle, and she'd run the kitchen while Belle ran the dining room. Maybe she could slip in a trip to the bank, or her car payment would be two months behind. She'd use the drive-thru so she didn't have to run into the jerk at the bank. She grimaced at herself in the mirror.

The bell signaled the door opening. She did a one-eighty.

Oh god.

No. No. No, god, no. It was him.

And he seemed fresh and—

She looked down at the stains on her top from a plate that had slid off a tray, and had ended up retexturizing and recoloring her blouse. Red pasta sauce almost resembled a blossoming gunshot wound. And then there was her face. God.

Relax. He's here to see Belle. Yes, that's right. But he asked for you the other day. BY name. He said Ms. Sanchez.

Stupid damned voice. If shaking her head would shake it away she'd do that, but it wouldn't. And she'd look weird on top of nasty, grimy, and oily. She slunk toward the kitchen, avoiding eye contact, hoping that would keep him from noticing her. Six yards away. She had only six yards to go and she'd be free and clear.

Five.

Belle was giggling that cute giggle of hers, a tinkling little laugh. Forgetting or forgiving—or both—that he'd stood her up for dessert.

Four yards to go. Just four; surely she could make it.

His response to Belle, whatever it was, was low, and even though she wasn't going to look at them, Marissa would have sworn it sounded... intimate. Ugh. And worse, why did that bother her?

Three.

Oh, yes. Almost there. Almost.

Two.

"Ms. Sanchez? Marissa?" Him. God. Ugh. His voice. Double-ugh!

She whirled around. *Shit*. He was practically on top of her. When she turned, she was looking right at his chin. And a nice, tan, strong chin it was.

Marissa chanced a look into his eyes. Amusement? He was amused? What the hell?

Suddenly her embarrassment at her appearance took a back seat to her anger at his amusement. Did he think the way she looked was funny? Marissa took a deep breath. No, she wasn't going to react. She was going to keep it together. No more Bitch Marissa from the other day. Nice Marissa was here. Sort of. She hoped. Prayed, even.

She cleared her throat, hoping the pause would give

her a chance to compose. Or recompose. Or stay composed. Or something. Anything. "Yes?" And still, she squawked the word out. What was it about this man? Every time she talked to him, at least when she said *yes,* it came out in a croak.

CHAPTER 14

*H*e breathed her in. Though she had clearly worked hard, and sweated, she had a muskiness, a—he inhaled again—scent to her that reached deep down into his gut, maybe even lower. Her eyes flashed their angry green fire, and her jaw jutted out.

He fought to keep from kissing her, wondering what it would be like. Wondering what it would taste like. He was no stranger to some of the human actions, like intimacy. He'd studied the lessons the Asazi were taught about humans in preparation for a journey to Earth. But he'd always fought the impulse and fought the human emotions that drove it. Was this a mistake? Was sending him here to do this a very bad idea? He had graduated at the top of his class at the Elite Measures Academy.

Why was this happening to him? He was a soldier. He had no weaknesses. He gritted his teeth to keep his anger from raising his pulse. His shoulder blades ached where his wings demanded to be released. He feared his skin would glow in its natural state, and freak her out with its colors. Curse this mission. Would he have to leave the restaurant to keep from being discovered? Was he such a failure?

He tore his gaze away from her lips, her face, held his breath and took a step back. "Ms. Sanchez." He released the breath slowly, regulating his pulse, regaining control of his faculties and his senses, his body. Somewhat. Yes, somewhat in regards to the body. That was harder to control.

Why didn't he have these reactions to the very, very willing Belle? Why? Why only this female? Why not the guest clerk at the hotel?

He wanted to call his cousin and ask him if this was normal. Then again, what if they yanked him from the mission? What if they removed him from the military? Or even worse, assigned him to a desk job? No, he would not allow that. Never.

Would they make him be Bound to Alithera again? Could they? Under what threat?

He put on what he'd practiced as his best smile. "I was hoping to have a visit with you, Ms. Sanchez. Do I need to set up an appointment for that?"

An expression passed over her face. It was fleeting,

but he would have sworn that it was vulnerability. What was that about?

Her shoulders slumped, almost as if she was admitting defeat. Defeat for what? What was going on in that head of hers? Suddenly and without understanding why, Finn wanted to know everything about this woman. What made her happy, what made her sad, mad, why she seemed defeated, why she'd been angry earlier. What she'd been like as a little human girl. What she liked to do for fun. Humans did a lot of that —fun stuff. The Asazi were not a fun-based culture. Theirs was based on different values. Of course, it had had to be. They had been transplanted to a new world long ago. There had been no time for luxury. And now that they were in danger of a dwindling population—

She was talking to him. What had she said? "I'm sorry. Could you repeat that?" He didn't want to tell her why. Especially since it was because he'd been daydreaming while she was talking.

"An appointment for what? Who are you? Who do you represent?" Her eyes narrowed, as though suspicion had overtaken her fatigue and defeat.

"Represent? I'm a scout. Simply that." This was all he could think to say. Pathetic. His plans for getting close to her vanished.

He was worthless. *A scout?* He could imagine Kal's voice already. *That was the best you could come up with?* Now Finn was happy there wasn't a transmitter in his phone or on his person that would relay their conversations, his blunders.

Or was there? No, surely they'd have told him. They wouldn't risk that anyway, would they? Risk humans finding out about Asazi by discovering alien instrumentation on them if they were captured? No. Surely not. But a niggling doubt remained.

Marissa cleared her throat and tapped her foot impatiently. "A scout for...?" Then another look passed over her face. It almost seemed like recognition, or acknowledgment. Whatever it was, it was quickly replaced with anger. She seemed angrier than she had been the last time they'd seen one another.

"You work for one of those damned vultures, don't you? One of those developers that wants me gone. Don't you? *Don't you?*" Her voice became louder and louder. Her face reddened. She was still a vision, but now she was a Valkyrie.

He took a step back, putting some distance between himself and her anger. "I'm not what you think. It's not what you think."

CHAPTER 15

*J*ust when Marissa was revving up, when she was ready to blast him with both barrels—

—the phone rang. And rang. And rang. And it dawned on her that Belle wasn't going to answer it. To compound the problem, Belle had a pleading look on her face, like she was beseeching Marissa to answer the phone so she could talk with this Finn guy. A guy Marissa was ready to kick out of her restaurant. Damned vulture.

She sprinted for the cordless. "Two West Two."

"Ms. Sanchez?"

That voice. Marissa's stomach felt like it was caught in a speedboat's propeller. *That ass from the bank.* She choked back her reflex to cuss the bastard out. "This is Marissa Sanchez."

"Ms. Sanchez, your failure to secure a loan—"

"Just get to the point."

"Ms. Sanchez." She could just imagine the sneer on his face. The same one he'd worn the last time they talked. "The sale of the property has been finalized. Effective at the end of the month, you will have to vacate the premises. You will receive formal notice via the sheriff's office today."

He probably wanted to gloat, but she bit that accusation back. "You can't do that. That's less than ten days away. I have rights."

"When your lease expired, you went month-to-month. Read your lease terms." *If you can read at all,* his tone implied.

The room closed in around her, getting smaller and smaller, darker and darker. She slumped into a booth, wishing she could sink into the upholstery.

Ten days. Ten days to erase all traces of Two West Two. "How am I supposed to do that? To move an entire restaurant in ten days? And where am I supposed to take everything?" She regretted the questions the minute they left her lips. She didn't want him to hear the pathetic desperation she felt. She pressed the *End Call* button and put her head between her hands, resting her forehead on the table's cool surface.

It was hard to breathe. For the first time in two years—*since Dad died*—she wanted a drink. A whole lot of a drink. That sounded like a winner, right about now.

"Marissa?" Belle's voice had a faraway quality.

"I don't feel very well. Can you call in some help? I —" Marissa rose, bracing her shaky legs by holding on to the table. "I—I'll see you later."

She picked up her bag from behind the register and made for the door. The man called Finn said something, but it was a low rumble and sounded more like a distant, muted thunder than words.

And then she was out in the blinding brightness of the afternoon. After slipping her sunglasses on, she fished her keys out of her pocket.

CHAPTER 16

And just like that—no notice, no clues, nothing —she was gone. The phone rang, she answered it. The call couldn't have been more than a minute, maybe two. Then she looked like a balloon that had had the air drained out of it. She laid her head on the table, then got up and grabbed her purse. She didn't respond to his question, didn't act like she'd heard it, or that he even existed. And then she was gone.

He wondered if he should let her go. He wondered if he should abort the mission altogether, maybe move on to the next target, because this one seemed so unpredictable.

Then the inexplicable happened. As if someone else was controlling his body, his mind, his actions, he found himself telling Belle he had to run an errand. And he followed her, this dark-haired, green-eyed woman with a warrior's spirit. He knew why he was doing it. He'd seen that look she had on her face. He'd seen it on shell-shocked soldiers who'd seen too much, lived through too much, and were numb. And numb soldiers did stupid things. Dangerous things.

Did female humans—women; Kal's word reverberated in his mind—did women do stupid things when they were numb or shell-shocked? He wished he'd paid better attention to some of the lessons. Right now, knowing more about humans would serve him better than knowing all the different techniques of killing, survival, espionage, evasion, reconnaissance, and escape. He slipped into the foot traffic, keeping enough of a distance behind her, and hoping she wouldn't notice him. Of course she wouldn't, he chastised himself. He was trained well. Sure, he argued with himself, but it hadn't taught him to evade discovery in a densely populated area.

As soon as he was home, as soon as this mission was complete, he would suggest to the Elite Measures Academy that they implement evasion in populated areas to their curriculum, but for now, he needed to pay better attention. To stay on his guard so she wouldn't notice him. Who knew how she'd react to his following her. If she had been mildly hostile earlier, now she might be outright antagonistic.

She stopped in front of her car, keys in hand. Then she shook her head, as if she was arguing with herself.

Her hair caught the sun's rays, a deep auburn tint in the dark waves. She turned around, a full revolution, and Finn stepped behind a light post, while maintaining an appreciative eye on the way she filled her jeans. She made a sharp 180 and headed down the street.

What was that about? What had that phone call meant? Belle had seemed concerned when Marissa told her to get help and run the dinner shift without her, as if this was not a commonplace event. As if Marissa never missed a day's work. Was she going somewhere to a business meeting? What kind of meeting would have her looking so defeated, so emotionless?

He walked behind her, keeping his distance varied, on occasion crossing the street as she trudged on, almost in a stupor. An hour later she stopped and surveyed her surroundings. He guessed they'd gone a good couple of miles from Two West Two. This was a far shabbier part of town, mostly dotted with bars, car repair shops, and homes with occasional bars across their windows. Those homes weren't in disarray. The ones that were in disarray, well—he supposed there was no reason to bar anyone from entering those.

She hurried across the street into a—

Finn looked for a sign. Anything that would identify the building. It wasn't a place of business, as far as he could tell.

A couple followed her in. Then another couple, holding hands. Odd. Maybe it was a business? But one that was unmarked? What sort of business would that be? The green door had no identifying marks, not even a street number. In her state of mind, probably not even paying attention, she'd be easy prey. He couldn't just let her be in there alone. Or maybe he was overreacting. Maybe he should go away.

And go where? There was nothing else for him to do, nowhere else for him to go. He had one mission. Marissa. Leaving her would mean he wouldn't be accomplishing his mission. Well, that and the fact that he didn't want to admit to himself that he wanted to be where she was. That in itself was too confusing to deal with. So what else was there to do but go in?

No, he'd wait and see if she came out. But first he had to make sure that there were no other exits. The building was two-story, whitewashed brick, with a metal staircase that led to the second floor on the outside. It had concrete steps and an ornate metal handrail.

A quick trip around the building assured him there were no windows. Odd, a building without windows. It used to have windows, but they'd been sealed with bricks.

Finn picked a spot across the street at a café and kept an eye on the green door. For more than an hour, no one came out, but four more laughing couples went in, along with a couple of unaccompanied women and one man.

Finn stretched in the chair, the human epidermis uncomfortable over his own skin in this heat. The sun was lowering, but not going down, not yet.

Maybe he should make an entrance, just to verify she was okay. *For the mission,* he told himself, knowing he wouldn't believe his own lie.

He crossed over and approached the door. Not even a peephole for security reasons. He tugged on the handle, and the door yielded without hesitation. Dimness greeted his eyes and took some adjusting to.

A bar.

This place was a bar. Jazz music drifted throughout the space, which was furnished with a collection of sofas and love seats. Candles and large, overstuffed chairs added to the ambience.

But no Marissa.

He made his way upstairs. More sofas. No bar. Couples were sitting on the sofas, but no one who was unaccompanied. Had he missed those? Where were they?

He skimmed down the steps, two at a time. Around the corner. There she was. Her back was to him, but she was in front of the bar's mirror with a drink in her hand.

He stepped back quickly, but not quickly enough. She frowned at his image in the mirror, as if to be sure she wasn't seeing things, and turned around.

She scratched her head, almost childlike in her

action. He knew what that meant, though he hoped it didn't mean what he thought it did.

"Finn."

Her slurred word confirmed it. She was drunk.

"You're following. You. Are. Following." She took a drink. "Me."

He didn't know what to say. If he confirmed it, would she accuse him of being a stalker? Would the bartender call the cops? That would be ugly. If he denied it, she'd know the truth.

"I was concerned." Might as well go with the truth.

"About me? Little ol' me?" She set the drink down, and it splashed up, clearly a hard landing. "You're a scout. For one of those developers." A sneer marred her features.

He was confused. What developers? Did he want to let her know he didn't know what she was talking about? Might as well, since her thinking he was a scout for a developer wasn't working out too well for him. "I don't know what you mean. What developers?"

She drew back, exaggeratedly so, almost theatrical. The stunned expression that replaced the sneer would have been funny, if the circumstances weren't the same, if she didn't hate him without a reason. "What do you mean, *what developers?* You don't know? You didn't— Belle didn't—you—"

Evidently she wasn't going to assemble a sentence that made sense, so he would have to take the lead. "I don't know what you're talking about. I left right after you did. You didn't seem to be okay."

"And you were worried about me."

"We've already established that." He pushed her drink away. She'd had enough and was too difficult to communicate with.

She brought it closer, took the straw between her teeth. The fluid rose through the opaque straw. She closed her eyes as she drank. If she weren't getting on his nerves with her incomprehension, he'd have been—

—cancel that thought. Too late—

—he *was* aroused. Very much so.

Cursed woman. Her cheeks hollowed as she sucked on the straw, and damn if his body didn't have a surge of electricity flowing through it. Thoughts ran rampant through his mind. Thoughts and a visual. And just like that—*wham!*—his wings pushed up against the human skin. He hoped they wouldn't pop through. That's all he needed. Functional or not, his wings wouldn't go unnoticed, even in a dark bar.

He shifted away, hoping that everything would subside. He hadn't spent much time in this body and it was already controlling him. In return, it threatened results that were uncontrollable.

"Oh, now you're mad?" Her head was cocked, one eyebrow raised, green eyes gleaming in the dancing candlelight.

"No, but I am wondering what this developer business is all about."

"Don't worry about it. So if you're a scout, but you don't work for a developer, then..." She swirled the straw around and around in the glass, the ice tinkling a soft jingle. Her eyes followed the tiny whirlpool created by the straw. In a flash, her head popped up, her eyes wide, like she'd seen something. Or knew something. "I get it. You're a talent scout. A headhunter for restaurants? Looking for managers?"

He took a second to evaluate an answer. She didn't seem to be appalled by that idea; in fact, she seemed pleased by it, as if it wasn't a bad thing. As if it might actually be a good thing.

"Yes." He tried to keep his tone confident, as if this was the truth. He raised himself taller on the stool. "That's exactly right."

She sank into a more relaxed pose.

He didn't exhale in relief, not wanting her to know, but he felt his pulse going back to normal along with his passion, and with it his wings retracted.

CHAPTER 17

It was as if suddenly everything was better. Except, the room was spinning. Okay, so maybe not everything. And her tummy wanted to spew its contents. Which for now were purely liquid. *So much for a liquid diet.* But at least this guy wasn't one of the enemies. That would have sucked. She didn't want to dwell on why it would have sucked. That would mean dwelling on something else. But who wanted another enemy when things were as bad as they were?

Could he be the answer to a problem? A job? Ugh. *Get it together, Marissa. You still have Two West Two.* Really? She wanted to rail at the whisper in her head. *I won't in ten days. If I don't come up with a plan I won't have enough capital to open up another restaurant.* Her head started to pound, thinking of it all. She wanted a drink, or twelve. Not to think about the future; to slip into a nice, inebriated little state. One where she didn't need to deal with life for a few hours.

He had to follow her here, just had to, didn't he? And now she was thinking about everything, and suddenly she wanted to drink more. She raised her glass to the bartender and nodded.

Then she saw it. Was that for real? In the reflection of the mirror, this guy—Finn, and what kind of name was *Finn*, anyway?—was shaking his head at the bartender, as if he could tell him not to make her another drink. She was a grownup, dammit. Who the hell did he think he was?

She turned to him so fast her head felt like it was going to pull a Linda Blair move. And never stop spinning. She placed her fingertips on her temples but still the room was swimming. Or maybe she was swimming. Wait, that wasn't possible.

"I don't feel so good. Why are you here again? Are you my guardian angel? Wait, wait. Angels have wings. You don't—" She pushed his stool, trying to swivel it, pretending to look for wings.

But his face changed. It went from sexy and sweet to—

Aloof.

Forbidding.

Like he was someone different altogether.

She drew back. Something was wrong. He jerked away, returned his seat to facing her. "Don't be silly."

"Jeez. It's a joke. Aren't you overreacting a little?" She reached for her drink. The glass was empty. She hunted for the bartender, but he was gone, before he'd gotten her a refill. How convenient.

"Maybe you're right. Maybe I am your wingless guardian angel. Don't you think you should let me take care of you if I am?"

"Um, no. You're still a stranger, guardian angel or not."

The seat felt like it was spinning. Or maybe it was the room. Whatever it was, the flavor of Kahlua and cream flowed in her throat, but very definitely from the wrong direction. White Russians didn't taste as good coming back up. She swallowed the liquid down.

No. No. No. That was the wrong thing to do. Now it was worse. Her stomach heaved. A glance up confirmed that Finn was watching her, concern on his face. She turned away from him. If she didn't, she'd—

God, too late. Just as she turned away, six White Russians projectile-erupted from her mouth. In her peripheral vision she caught his jump backward, and his barstool flipped, clipping hers just right.

Marissa tumbled to the floor, vomit cascading around her. She slipped on the nasty, grimy, chunky floor and landed right on her ass.

CHAPTER 18

Marissa, the human firebrand, was vomiting a white-ish concoction in his direction. He made a swift flip out of her way, but he didn't count on his barstool tipping, or knocking hers over. He sure didn't count on her falling down and her own vomit pelting her.

She sat on the floor, this forlorn, former firebrand, lost, covered in her own vomit, miserable. Pitiful.

Now what? Fueled by alcohol, and embarrassment, what would her temper lead her to do? He paused, waiting for her reaction. The other thing he hadn't counted on—

A flood of tears burst from her eyes, while her face maintained no emotion at all. This woman was beyond confusing. He leaned in, hoping she'd accept his help.

Help? Help her do what? What could he do? The

only way to give this woman help would be to throw her in a bathtub. Preferably one filled with cold water to shock the alcohol's effects out of her body and bring her to her senses. What could he say that would make anything better? Nothing. So he put his hand out to help her up.

She stared at his hand like it was a cobra.

What was wrong with her? "Let me help you."

"I'm beyond help." The snot dribbling from her nose merged with the tears.

He was happy she was too drunk—hopefully too drunk—to remember the sight she was. With luck, tomorrow morning she wouldn't have any inkling of this performance.

And why did that matter, anyway? In a short time, she'd become a part of the mission to help his people.

What would they do to her? Or to any of the women? What exactly happened once they were in Asazi custody? He should have asked. Why? Why would he have asked? It wasn't his business. His assignment was to bring them in. He wasn't a scientist. But now, suddenly, this woman made him want to know. To know that she'd be okay. To know that she wouldn't come to harm. To know she'd still be that human spitfire, not a corpse. Or even an incubator.

What was wrong with him? Why did he care? Was it the human genomes in his body that made him care? Or was it the fact he'd taken on a human appearance?

What was going on? He leaned back, fighting to keep his confusion, and concern, from showing on his face.

"Hey, bud." The bartender was back and tugging on Finn's sleeve. "She's a nice lady, and a good tipper and all that." His face grew concerned as he looked down at Marissa. "But you're going to have to... well, she's drunk. You're going to have to take your girlfriend out of here."

"She's not—" Before Finn could say *She's not my girlfriend*, the bartender raised his hand in the universal *Halt* gesture.

"She is drunk. She's definitely drunk."

That wasn't what Finn was going to dispute. A person would have to be deaf, blind, and have no sense of smell to dispute that Marissa was drunk. He nodded in agreement.

The bartender continued. "She's going to cause me trouble with the law."

"How so?" This was out of Finn's area of expertise.

"Public intoxication, blah, blah, blah. Whatever. What I need you to do is get her out of here."

"I don't think she can walk, and her house is quite a distance away."

"Yeah, man, I called a cab for her."

That seemed to settle the matter. Finn lifted her, cradled her head under his chin, and held his breath so he wouldn't have to inhale the combination of cream, Kahlua, vodka, and stomach bile. "Let's go, Marissa, honey." That was for the benefit of the bartender, since Finn was going to be taking her home... or was he? At least he had to go along with the bartender's theory that he was her boyfriend. He carried her to the door, the bartender flicked the knob, and Finn kneed it open the rest of the way. Sure enough, a cab was waiting outside.

Seeing Finn, the cabbie came around and opened the door. "I've been here a few minutes. The meter's been running." His accent was thick, his smile broad and even-toothed under a knit cap.

"Thanks. No problem. I understand about the meter."

Marissa moaned but didn't open her eyes as he set her in the seat, careful not to jostle her too much, and still very careful not to breathe in too deeply. That odor—not pleasant.

"Where to, brother?" The cabbie looked in the rearview mirror.

Luckily Finn had no problem remembering her address. Good thing he'd taken this seriously and had learned the details in her file. "1483 Feather Hollow."

The cabbie put the car in gear and nosed it out of the parking lot. And still Marissa gave no indication of waking up. She was out for the whole trip. Not a long trip, less than twenty minutes' drive to leave that area of town and progress to a part that was better kept up. A whole lot better kept up. Suburbia, pretty much.

En route, Finn took her keys out of her purse and pocketed them. It'd make opening a door easier if he didn't have to dig through the purse while carrying a passed-out-Marissa to her front doorstep. He paid the driver, tipped him well, took Marissa out.

The door yielded to the key without issue, but he didn't push it open. He stopped to listen, to be sure there wasn't a dog. The last thing he needed was to have to fend off—or worse, kill—her dog. That'd be hell to explain to her when she came to, later. Explanations would be the easy part. The hate she'd have for him—that was something he didn't want to think of.

He waited a full three minutes. Scuffled a little, made some noise. No barking, no growling, no canine toenails skittering on wood or tile. Finn pushed the door open and was greeted by a small lamp's light. Thankfully because otherwise, he'd have tripped over the pile of junk that sat just to the left of the door, almost barring his entrance. "Damn, it's an obstacle course," he muttered under his breath.

Marissa shifted in his arms. "What?"

"Nothing. Go back to sleep."

"Dad? Daddy?"

He froze. Her father had died about two years ago. Her file said so, and he doubted it wasn't accurate. So why was she calling out to her dad? "Shhh. Just rest." He pressed her face closer to his chest. Just a couple minutes longer and he could put her in her own bed and—

And what? What after that, genius? Wait until morning? Wait until she wakes up, crusty from her own vomit and—

And then she'd never want to talk to him again. She'd be mortified, ashamed, embarrassed. He knew that already. He knew her. He couldn't have her waking up and finding herself a mess, then finding out he'd brought her here, that he'd seen her at her lowest.

He'd have to do something. Make it seem like she'd come home, changed, something, anything, but he couldn't let it look like he'd seen her in this condition.

No problem. You're a soldier. Surely you can handle this. Her chest rose in a sleep-sigh, her breasts pushing tight against her clothing.

He shouldered a couple of doors open, then finally found her master bedroom. He placed her on the bed, secured a washcloth from the adjoining bathroom, moistened it with some warm water, and, using the light cast by the bathroom, he unbuttoned her wet, messy top. Between the vomit, the chunks, and what looked like she'd had a red sauce food fight during lunch, the shirt deserved a fiery funeral. He balled it up and tossed it in a corner.

In the dim lighting, her flesh glowed, tan with white lines from a swimsuit. A lacy contraption—a bra, that much he remembered—covered half her breasts, leaving little to the imagination. Her nipples pressed against the filmy fabric. He sucked a breath in as quietly as he could. Her breasts rose, fell, rose, fell with every inhale and exhale. He found his own breathing matching hers as he stared at her, transfixed by the creamy, glowing skin. His shoulders ached, and he knew why. Damned wings. Damned humans.

The bra was wet. Leave her in it or...?

He rummaged through a few drawers and found an oversized T-shirt. Rolling her to her side, he unhooked the contraption holding her breasts hostage then tugged it off. It felt like a bayonet was being driven through his gut. Her curves invited him, and he raised his hand, lowered it. He couldn't. No. This couldn't happen.

Taking the washcloth, he ran its warmth moistness over her neck, her chest and just over the curve of her breast. As he passed it over her nipple, it turned stiff. He let his thumb touch it. Damnation, he couldn't help himself. He swallowed the thickness that had accumulated in his throat, and adjusted the discomfort growing in his pants. Her nipple pressed back against his thumb. He wanted to taste it. Vomit, sweat, all of that be damned.

He leaned in, imagining the texture in his mouth. Imagining its response to his sucking.

She gasped, took a deep breath and rolled over onto her side.

Saved. To think he was going to—

He shook his head, as if that would clear it. As if that would make a difference. Fool. Foolish human blood in his body. He stood and paced. Now what? Now?

It's fine, he reassured himself. *She doesn't know. She knows nothing. She—*

All he had to do was put her shirt on her, cover her, go to her couch, and go to sleep. She'd wake up in the morning and be none the wiser. She'd assume she'd dressed herself and that he was the perfect chaperone.

He slipped the T-shirt over her body, covered her and slipped out, leaving the door cracked open. Then he leaned against the wall just outside the door, and stared out the window at the moonless, cloudless sky.

What am I doing? What have I done?

What was I going to do?

CHAPTER 19

*H*er head felt like it was going to explode. She knew that feeling. Knew it well, though it had been forever since she'd last felt it. Marissa groaned and pulled the pillow over her face. The sun. Brutal! The night before was a dim fog of a memory, but she knew she'd gone to Hush last night. She'd—

Marissa bolted upright.

Finn.

She scanned her bed. There definitely weren't any signs of a wild, passionate night. Or a hot guy.

What was she thinking? She wasn't the type. She didn't do stuff like that. *No, not normally,* the voice reminded her. *But he was hot. And you were drunk.* Still, she didn't—

No, she hadn't. The room was unoccupied. She was

in her night T-shirt, and the other half of the bed was untouched. And she was pretty sure no parts of the bed would have been untouched if he'd been here.

What the hell is wrong with me? She was acting like a whacked out, hormonal, horny...

She buried her face in the pillow and laughed at herself.

A knock interrupted her.

God. That sounded close. The door crept open. "Marissa?"

Him. Oh. Him. Finn. OhOhOh. Oooooh.

She jerked the sheets up to her neck. "Yes?" Back to the pretty-much-a-croak-while-he-was-around sound. Shit.

"Just checking on you."

"Oh. I'm—" What the hell was he doing here? "I'm okay. I don't remember much of last night."

"No problem. We shared a cab. I stayed to make sure you were okay." He pushed the door all the way open. "You were under the weather."

Marissa fought back a laugh at that understatement and at the same time prayed that she hadn't acted stupid, that she hadn't done anything embarrassing. And, in the same breath, she fought the urge to stare at him. His hair was tousled. His face had that just right amount of scruff that would leave red marks on her thighs while he—

God. Stop this train of thought. Right now, Marissa Sanchez. Right this moment!

His eyes... Dark, black, the iris and pupils merging into one mysterious black hole that threatened to suck her in.

He was shirtless and had a huge tattoo of a winged —what was that?—on his huge bicep.

Stop. Immediately.

But she didn't want to stop. She looked out the window, looked at anything she could to keep from looking at this man in rumpled clothes, the man with the bedroom eyes that she wanted to dive into.

"What? What were you saying?" She'd completely lost track of what he'd said.

A glimmer of amusement crinkled his eyes. "I was saying I hope you feel better. I'll get you breakfast if you like. I presume a lady who owns a restaurant would have a stocked pantry."

He would lose that bet for the most part, but the part that got her was, how did he know she owned a restaurant? *Quit being paranoid, Marissa. You probably told him last night, while you were too busy drowning your problems instead of handling them.* Or Belle could have.

"Belle! Shit." Marissa jumped up. "Two West Two. Oh God. I'm such an idiot." She'd left and... who had run the shift? Who had managed the restaurant? God, she was pathetic. Then she noticed her breasts bouncing in her tee. Her bra? What had happened to it?

She didn't usually take it off. Where? Ah, there it was, at the foot of the bed. She looked away so Finn wouldn't catch her looking, and she crossed her arms so he wouldn't notice the bouncing her breasts were doing when she hurled herself up out of the bed.

Then it hit her: Two West Two was going to close in ten days anyway. What did one shift matter? It wasn't like it was a legacy that she was leaving behind. It would soon be nothing, less than a memory. She turned away so Finn wouldn't see the tears in her eyes.

"Hey."

"Yeah." She tried to keep from sounding like she was crying.

His arms were on her shoulders, pulling her close, swiveling her to face him. "Belle called. I answered your phone. Hope that was okay. She said she ran the shift and that everything went smoothly. She said you're closed today? Every Sunday and Monday? Is that correct?"

"Yeah. And it was pathetically irresponsible for me to do what I did last night. Uncalled for."

"Based on what I heard from Belle, I'd say, very called for. You're human, after all." His tone had an oddness to it when he said that. "Do you have a plan?"

"I guess I'll put the restaurant supplies and equipment in an auction to see if I can't raise some money. It won't be enough to open up another one, but it'll give me some money to live on until I find another job."

"Why don't you get back in bed? I'll get breakfast and coffee. How do you take it?"

"Cream, lots of it. No sugar. But you don't have to." She made to pull away from his hold, but his grasp was firm, not overly so, not forcing her, but like he was a rock she could hold on to.

Then he was gone, and she was alone in her bedroom, and suddenly it felt like the loneliest place in the world. Since when did this guy matter? Since when did his leaving a room leave her empty? What had happened last night? Surely nothing.

She looked at her bra. She usually slept with it on. It was more comfortable that way. She picked it up. Still damp. She didn't need to put it under her nose to smell the reek of vomit.

Must have taken it off because it was wet and filthy. Had to be.

But still a part of her wondered, even wished. *Wow, you do sound like a girl who needs to get laid.* Now she wanted to tell the voice to fuck off. But what was the point of that?

She brushed her teeth and warmed the water in the shower. That would hit the spot. And make things smell better. After tossing her filthy shirt, bra, night tee, jeans and panties into the hamper, she jumped into the hot water. She closed her eyes and let the water run down her body. The scent of her body gel filled the steamy air as she ran her hands over her breasts. Her nipples hardened under her fingertips. For a moment she thought of Finn, his hands, his mouth. Damn it. What was wrong with her? That was the last thing she needed to be doing right now, thinking of him. She rushed through her shower.

CHAPTER 20

He paced the kitchen, pausing to take in the black, silver, and red décor. The whole house had furniture in bold, stark, crisp lines, including the kitchen. The Asazi part of his mind relished the order and unchaotic nature of the house.

Why the hell had he done that? Why had he told her he'd make breakfast? And coffee? *Since when have you ever used a human appliance?* By the Asazi Sacred Writings, he was becoming more and more stupid every moment. It would be a miracle if the humans didn't capture and kill him, or examine him with a scalpel and a microscope. Damned fool. Damned, damned fool. Yes he would be damned. Damned and sentenced to die in this chaotic, frantic world, while at home everyone wondered what had happened to him. He might as well slink away and find somewhere to take his own life and destroy his body so as not to leave any evidence.

But there was one problem. He wasn't a quitter.

He stopped and took stock. Mr. Coffee. Well, that would be where one made coffee, wouldn't it? He would worry about the cooking part later. Cooking? Asazi men didn't cook. Not the ones who became soldiers, anyway. And most of them did. They had to have more soldiers than anything else. Soldiers, medics, and morticians. Soldiers to fight off the intermittent invaders, medics to heal the soldiers, and morticians for the rest.

He took a step closer to Mr. Coffee and grabbed the handle of a glass jar on top of a metal plate. He understood that part. The metal would be a conductor for heat, but... what about the coffee? Where did that come from?

Lifting the black lid on the top, he wondered if that was where one put coffee. Wait, he needed to find coffee. From the other room, the sound of water streaming bought him some time. Hopefully she was the type who liked to spend a lot of time in the washing and grooming stages. That might give him enough time to figure out where the coffee was and how to cook it. He opened cupboard drawers and doors with as much stealth as he could. Somewhere—there!—the label said coffee. Yes! Coffee Mate? What did that mean? A brand of coffee? He pried the lid open. White powdery coffee? Who was he to question advances in Earth's science? He poured a healthy amount of the powder into the top of the coffee-maker, stepping back as a tiny white mushroom cloud formed.

Then he heard it. The water cut off. Time to hurry. Now what? He filled the remainder of the container with water. A red button with a 1 and a 0 on it... of course. He pressed the button and took a step back, fairly proud of himself. His mind went to his grandmother again, and how she used to smile when he did things that humans did. That should do it. And what about the glass container? Did that go on the Mr. Coffee machine? Or... He thought of the girl at the coffee shop last night, who had put a cup under the spout that made the coffee concoctions. He fumbled around in the cabinets, found a mug and set it on the metal plate. Within seconds a stream of hot, white liquid made its way out of the tiny spouts on the underside of Mr. Coffee's tank.

And now for breakfast. She would be screwed if he was making it. How could he get out of that? He couldn't. So he rummaged through the refrigerator, hoping whatever he was going to make didn't have to be prepared on the stove. Surely there were foods that would be ready, like the way it was in the Asazi world. One button, and a meal was being pushed through the chute for the recipient.

The refrigerator was nearly empty. How could that

be? How could someone who owned a restaurant not have a kitchen full of food?

Maybe offering to take her to breakfast would be a better idea. But then would she want to go their separate ways? Perhaps cooking something for her here would make her hate him less? Though this morning she didn't seem to hate him as much. In fact, for a second, he would have sworn he saw hunger in her eyes. Of course that had been chased away by embarrassment when she noticed that her breasts were bouncing. What she probably hadn't noticed was the way the peaks, rosy and poking against the fabric, were tempting him to—

Get your mind off of that. Now. This is pointless.

He turned the burner on the stove. Nothing happened. Nothing except a hissing sound. Maybe that was normal? Maybe a stove hissed so that the person cooking would know it was on? But where was the heat? He touched the silver circles. Nothing. He hovered his hand over the four circular areas. No heat. Odd. Maybe it didn't work.

He'd go ask her. Or should he?

A loud bumping knock from down the hall, in the direction of her room, answered that. Worried she might be hurt, he sprinted the few yards and pushed the door open with his forearm.

Sacred Writings in stone and blood!

She was naked, leaning over a chair that had fallen.

She jumped up, fallen chair forgotten. What he couldn't ignore was the sight that had greeted him. A firm, round ass, curvy, parted just enough to see a glimpse of—

She screamed. "What are you doing?"

"I heard a noise." He turned his head away, kept his gaze down. "I wasn't sure you were unhurt. It seemed loud from the kitchen."

"You can look now."

Was she inviting him? To—

He turned her way. Oh, she was covered. *That's what she meant.*

Marissa wrinkled her nose. "What's that smell?"

"I don't know. Not familiar. Maybe it's the coffee?"

"No, it smells like gas. Is the burner—" She took off for the kitchen, wrapped in a sheet that trailed behind her.

He ran after her, not sure why she thought the kitchen would smell like gas. He'd been by the gas station, and this smell was nothing like that.

"What the hell happened here?" Her hand was over her mouth, the sheet slipping on one side.

"I made coffee." He looked at the Mr. Coffee. The problem was, the white coffee had overflowed the cup and was surrounding the coffee-maker in an ivory pool.

"Oh my god. The burner." She turned the knob on

the stove. "Why was this on?" She scanned the counters. "There isn't even any food out."

"I was going to make you breakfast." He could feel the anxiety building in him. He was such a failure at this mission. Stupid, nonsensical mission. And just as quickly, his pulse escalated, and his wings pushed up against his shoulder blades.

"What's up with the coffee machine? What's this white crap?" She opened a drawer and took out a towel, popped open the lid on Mr. Coffee and peered inside. "You put creamer in here? Tell me you didn't do that."

"I didn't. I put Coffee Mate." He grabbed another towel and began the process of sopping up the white liquid as quickly as he could, hoping to erase all residue evidence of his failings. Give him a weapon and he would rule, but this domesticated human stuff—failure. He shoved the towel into the white mess.

"You—" She gave him a strange look. Like maybe he'd lost his mind. "You put creamer in there. Coffee Mate. Creamer." As if she was talking to a baby.

He wanted to hope she wasn't saying that what he'd put in there wasn't coffee. But he knew that was exactly what she was saying.

"What were you thinking? Are you okay? Do you know how to make coffee?" She tossed the first towel in the sink and grabbed another.

That one he could answer truthfully. "No, I don't."

She paused her wiping and looked up at him, green eyes wide, mouth in an O. "You've never made coffee? Ever?"

He put his finger under her chin to close her mouth. "No." He was getting angry. Angry at himself for messing everything up. Angry at Kal for sending him here. Angry at this girl for—

What was he angry with her for? Angry that he couldn't control his pulse around her, that's what. And that was just for starters. He angled himself away from her, in case the wings erupted enough to be noticeable under his shirt. Damn, she'd call the police if that happened. Then he'd be in a heap of trouble.

"Something weird is going on here." She backed up and put her hand close to a wooden block with several knife handles spiking out like sentries.

"Weird how?" He backed up, anything to keep her from thinking he was dangerous. Anything to keep her from reaching for a weapon. He'd have to kill her. That would make his mission a failure.

No, that wasn't what was bothering him. He couldn't imagine those green eyes not lit up, not on fire.

"Your skin. It—" She rubbed her eyes. "I think I'm seeing things. Your skin was just—I swear, it looked like it was a glowing, shimmering orange color."

He forced a laugh, hoping it came out authentic. "Orange? I think you had too much to drink last night."

Her giggle was sheepish; so was the look on her face. Still, a cute little laugh. She walked to the counter on the other side of the kitchen and sat on a barstool, put her elbows on the counter and her head in her hands. "It's been a day. Week. Life."

"Are you okay?" Great. Just great. Now he'd asked her to bring him into her life. He'd start to care and—

Who are you kidding? You already care. Damn that conscience, or whatever that was. But it was right. He did care about her. How could he have come to care about a woman he'd known for only 24 hours? He looked at the kitchen clock, a silver square without numbers on it, with hands that were shaped like elongated triangles. No, less than twenty-four hours. In two hours it would be twenty-four hours since he'd first entered Two West Two.

She shook her head, still in her hands. "Nah, I'm not that okay, but it doesn't matter. I'll figure it out."

He took a step closer, hoping to console her, anything to make her feel better, but the sheet slipped with the headshake. And then slipped lower, exposing creamy skin and the edge of one rosy nipple.

If he told her about it, then she'd think he was a pervert for looking. At the same time, he didn't want to take his eyes off her body. He turned away and focused on the greenery outside the kitchen window, but he couldn't get the image out of his mind. She'd probably think he was cold for not acknowledging her distress, but—

Curses. He couldn't just let her sit there in pain and not comfort her. He turned her way and without casting a single glance below her neck, he put his hands on her bare shoulders. Her skin gleamed in the morning sunlight, and her flesh was warm to his hand.

Goosebumps rose beneath his fingertips. Still sitting, she raised her eyes to his, her lower lip trapped between her teeth.

Finn traced the curve of her lip with his thumb, releasing it from her teeth. Her eyes left his, travelling down his chest, then lower. In his pants, the same reaction tugged at him, reminding him how much he wanted her.

She raised a brow, then looked him in the eye again. Her chest was unmoving, like she was holding her breath.

CHAPTER 21

She couldn't believe where her thinking was going. She found herself wanting to give in to all the naughtiness she'd always dreamed of yielding to but never had. Her life had always been so PG-13, and now she wanted to elevate it to triple X, completely bypassing anything in between. She wanted to unbuckle his pants and see him, feel him. Even taste him.

His thumb was still on her lip. She lowered her head and took it in her mouth, sucking on it. He moaned, and his chest swelled with a deep breath. Marissa put a hand on his stomach, then raised it toward his chest.

With a sweeping move he picked her up under her arms and placed her on the countertop. The sheet dropped with the motion. He sucked in a breath just as the sheet fell.

Marissa didn't care she was naked, didn't care that she was probably a hungover-looking mess. None of that mattered.

His eyes were focused on her breasts. Her nipples peaked and hardened under his glance, wanting to be touched. Her breathing shallowed, and still the man did nothing but stare at her.

"Finn." His name was almost a whisper on her lips; she couldn't manage much more than that. "Don't just stare at me. Please. Can you—" What was she thinking? Was she really going to ask him to touch her?

He took a foot in each hand, raised her feet and put her heels on the counter. The undertaking spread her legs. Cool air passed over her heated dampness. He stared between her legs, his tongue moistening his lips. It was innocent, but so suggestive. Marissa put her hands behind his head and fought the urge to give it the tiniest pull forward. Lord, she wanted this man so much. Wanted to feel him on her, around her, in her.

Finn traced his fingers from her heel, up her calf, under her knee, around and on the inside of her thigh, his movements slow, deliberate, gentle. Deep within, Marissa's muscles flexed in response. His fingers stopped at her folds, pressed down, then drew her open.

At the burst of coolness on her inner folds and wet

center, a gasp ripped from her lungs and her head flew back, tapping the cabinet behind her.

Finn lowered his head, his breath warm on the same areas that had just cooled. She held her breath, waiting, wanting, knowing, and yet knowing nothing at all.

CHAPTER 22

*H*er face was flushed as her hands applied the tiniest pressure behind his head, pressing him closer to the place he wanted to be. Her skin was cool, and there were goosebumps on her flesh as he traced the contours of her legs, her thighs, until finally reaching her dark, rose-colored folds. He touched the fleshiness, enjoying the way she contracted under his touch, and spread her open, juices evident at her entrance.

He breathed her in, savoring the scent of her, the essence of this human female, this woman. He bent his head closer and closer, going slowly, giving her a chance to push him away, the whole time absorbing her scent and wondering if her taste matched it.

When she didn't push him away, driven to distraction by his shaft pulsing a primal beat, he lowered his head, touching the tip of his tongue to the tiny button he'd exposed. Beneath his fingertips, her flesh quivered, her legs opening wider.

Wondering what would please her, he covered her clit with his mouth and sucked gently, basing his rhythm and pressure on her reactions.

He released her clit and ran his tongue downward, allowing it to slip inside the slightest bit on the return journey.

"I can't believe this." Her voice was sex-rough, a tortured whisper.

He raised his head, her essence on his tongue. "Shall I stop?"

"Oh, god, no. It's just... this isn't who I am. Is it?" She ran her fingers over her face, through her hair. "I barely know you."

"I feel like I've always known you. And yet—"

"I know. I know." Her breathing was rapid, hasty. "It's the same for me. But still—"

Wracked by confusion, still tasting her, Finn came to a decision that his throbbing member protested against. The Asazi part of his brain had ceased to exist. It was his lust and his emotions that ruled now. And then suddenly, something defeated the Asazi part that wasn't working and even defeated the lust that threatened to overtake him. He shifted away, put his hands on her knees, closed her legs, and helped her off the counter.

Asazi curses and damnation! This was hard, walking away from her, from her scent, taste, feel. He battled to control his lust.

With a gentle kiss on his mind, he placed his lips on hers. Her mouth parted, and his tongue acted of its own volition, entering, exploring, reaching, doing all the things it had wanted to do below.

He cupped her breast, his thumb twirling the hardened button, rolling it between his thumb and finger, amazed by the instant response. Her breast swelled in his palm. Her chest rose and fell at a rapid rate.

He took a half-step back, retrieved her sheet and reluctantly wrapped it around her. "You go get dressed, I'll clean the kitchen up, and we'll go to breakfast. My treat. What else do you have to do? You have two days off. You may as well enjoy one of them. Who knows, I may be able to help you solve a problem or two."

Her laugh was wry, but she stood and headed down the hall, sheet bunched in her fist, covering all of the parts he'd love to see in greater detail—explore, taste, savor.

CHAPTER 23

What was wrong with her? Marissa closed the door to her bedroom, leaned against it, knees weak. She could taste her flavor on his mouth. She licked her lips, the desire to be with him refusing to subside.

She didn't need to be going to breakfast with him. She needed to be—

Needed to be what? It wasn't like she could do what she normally did. Her life trajectory had suddenly tangented in a whole new direction. *Yeah, a direction that sucks. No job, no nothing.* Her father would be very disappointed in her, that she was losing Two West Two.

As if you haven't wanted to leave it for the last few years. As if you weren't tired of the restaurant business. Okay, that was true. She was tired of it. She'd wanted to quit and sell the place a few years ago. And when she'd told Dad about it, he'd said, "Sell it. Get out of there. Go be happy."

Her response to her father had been that she felt an obligation to the community to keep it around. That it was the oldest restaurant in the area, and she couldn't just sell it. What if the new owners didn't care as much?

Her father had replied, "That's not your problem. Your customers are busy making themselves happy. You should do the same."

Yet some screwed-up sense of obligation had kept her there. For years. She wadded and threw the sheet on the bed, disgusted with herself. But there was a part of her, a secret part, that wanted to rejoice. She now could walk away from Two West Two and not feel guilty. She'd done her best, and circumstances outside of her control had put an end to this part of her life, an end to Two West Two. An end to obligation.

Responsible, duty-bound Marissa could relax and look into pursuing the things in life she'd wanted, but still she felt like she was being bad. *What the hell is wrong with me?*

Her stomach rumbled. *Okay, okay, I get the hint.* She grabbed a pair of jeans and a top and slipped into them. A puff of powder on her face, a touch of lip gloss, a couple of strokes of blush. That should do it.

Shit. Her hair. She shook it out, finger-styled it. Mentally proclaimed *What the hell* and went with it.

She switched the lights off and headed back to the kitchen to make sure that sexy hunk of a man called Finn wasn't burning anything down.

Finn. Why had she done what she'd done with him? Why was she going to breakfast with him? Why was she doing anything with him? Why wasn't she doing something productive? *Marissa, relax, jeez, for once stop and smell the roses.*

The kitchen was immaculate, the towels rinsed and laid out across the backs of the stools to air dry. Finn was leaning against the counter, arms folded across his chest, looking more like a Roman gladiator than a talent scout.

Talent scout. She definitely needed to explore that. If he was truly a headhunter for restaurants and hospitality-oriented corporations, she might have her next lead for a job.

"That was quick." His eyes took in her appearance, and suddenly Marissa felt like she was back in junior high, not quite measuring up to the pretty, popular girls. Oh, she knew she wasn't a double-bagger, but she wasn't like the cheerleaders either. *You didn't put out like they did, either.* Damned voice never let up, did it? So what if she hadn't been a skanky slut in high school? So what if the first guy she kissed had said she sucked at it? So what? Surely she'd improved since then? She touched her lips self-consciously, hoping that she—

Quit thinking like that. Quit it now. "Yes. I didn't want

to leave you waiting." Now she second-guessed her clothing. Maybe she should have dressed like someone who was looking for a job, someone who could manage a restaurant. *As if you managed this one? Your numbers were going downhill. That's because of the circumstances.* She had to stop this now. This doubt thing was killing her. "So where's your car?"

"I took a cab."

She looked out the window. "Where's mine?" Wow. She must have been wasted. Thank goodness she hadn't driven home. But had she driven to Hush?

"It's in front of Two West Two."

Of course it was. She should have remembered. That was where she'd left it when she'd stormed out, after that phone call. "Perfect. That's not a long walk from here. Truth be told, I shouldn't even drive to work every day, and yet..."

She didn't have a reason for driving instead of walking. Well, yes, she did. She carried enough stuff back and forth, including her purse, that it was more convenient. Not to mention that she didn't usually allow enough time in the morning for walking. Plus, she walked all day in the restaurant. And visited a gym. Yeah, she got plenty of exercise. *God, what is this, beat up on myself day? Justify everything I do day? Get off this track, Marissa Sanchez. Like right now.*

She squared her shoulders. It was time to go have fun. Time to be a different Marissa.

CHAPTER 24

She looked stunning, even with the effects the alcohol had to have had on her. "I know a breakfast spot down the road."

He couldn't risk a team coming for her. And if she was near the area... "No. Can we go... further?"

She cast him a sideways glance from behind the steering wheel. "Like where?"

"I'm not from this area. Isn't there somewhere scenic you can take me?"

"Scenic? In Houston?" Her brow furrowed, as if that wasn't likely. "Well, how about we go have breakfast in The Woodlands? There should be something nice up there. And it's a nice part of town."

"Do you not know of the eateries and scenic areas in Houston?"

"Yeah, I guess, but you see, I work in a restaurant.

And actually I work a lot of hours. So it's not like I go anywhere or do much." She shrugged. "But anyway, The Woodlands sounds good."

"How far is it from here?"

"About forty-five to an hour."

That should give them some distance from anyone hunting him. Or her. He reached into his pocket, took out the phone and turned it on. It signaled an email. From yesterday evening.

Kal. Worried about Finn. Wondering if his food supply was holding out. Warning him that things could happen if he ran out of Asazi food.

He'd been out for quite a while now, backpack at the restaurant, and had consumed more than a few human meals. And now he was going to have another one. And there'd been no adverse effects. Except for that thing in the hotel room, with the woman on the television, and a short time ago, with Marissa. But he didn't consider that to be adverse. Not adverse at all. It had been pleasurable.

But he wasn't going to tell Kal that, or about the food he'd been eating, and not eating.

He did wonder if human food was why his body had reacted the way it had to the television. And to Marissa. Mostly to Marissa now. It felt like the whole time he'd been around her, he'd had a buzzing in his veins, a throbbing in his loins. And he hadn't been able to get rid of it.

A thought struck him. "What direction is this Woodland place from here?"

She laughed, as if he'd said something funny. "*The* Woodlands. There are some people who get irate if you forget the THE. It's north from here. And east."

That wasn't quite good. The Asazi were set up north, but west. He thought they'd be better off going the opposite direction. "So what's south of here?"

"Galveston?" Her tone was perplexed.

"And past Galveston?"

Another laugh. He liked the way she laughed, though he remembered that not far beneath it there was an angry, passionate little hellion.

"Water. The Gulf Coast. Nothing, pretty much. Unless you can walk on water."

"No one can walk on water." He was confused by her statement.

"Never mind. But yes, just Galveston."

"Can we go there instead?"

"I'll make a U-turn. Hey, by the way, you left your backpack in my restaurant you know. Is there anything important in it?"

Kal would think so. "No. Nothing I can't live without." This seemed to be truer than he'd been told. If his team went there, they'd know he had been in her restaurant. They would know he wasn't eating Asazi food. They'd know he was eating human food. And whatever consequences they thought happened, they'd presume had.

They might start to put some things together, though he doubted they could put it all together. Like why he was with her and where they were going and why it was so damned important to him to save her.

Hell's curses, he couldn't figure that out himself. One thing he knew: he couldn't take her back to her home or to the restaurant. But he didn't know the why of that either.

CHAPTER 25

She should get her head checked. What kind of foolishness was this? Going anywhere with a stranger, in a car? A guy that size would have no problem taking care of her. No problem at all. *Sometimes I'm so stupid.*

But there was something about him. Something about his eyes, the set of his jaw. And it wasn't about the hotness factor, though heavens above, the man was some kind of hot. She took a sideways glance at his bicep, that chest. He'd have no problem containing her, if he meant her harm. But she trusted him. He had this... this thing about him, like he'd been hurt. He reminded her of a wounded wolf.

Two West Two was closed, and she really didn't have much to do. No social life. No business to worry about, since it wasn't going to be around much longer, was it? And he was hot.

Hot men get you in trouble.

Yeah, yeah, she didn't care about that right now. Plus, he was a headhunter. He could get her a job, or an interview at the very least. And if he really meant her any harm, he'd probably have done that last night.

She felt heat rising to her cheeks at the thought of his being here, about last night, how she'd come to be in different clothes. And most of all, at the stuff they'd done this morning. She didn't even want to go there right now.

The drive to Galveston usually seemed long, but with Finn next to her, it seemed to fly by. He wasn't overly talkative, so she turned on her playlist to keep from plaguing him with all the questions brewing in her head.

Almost an hour into the drive, after passing countless stretches of reed-covered, brackish water, a bridge or two, a strip club, and way more taco stands on the side of the road than there should be, she couldn't stand it anymore. She had to talk, to ask, to find out about him.

""Where are you from?" That seemed like a safe start.

A frown creased his forehead, but not for long. "Another country."

Keeping one hand on the wheel, she turned his way

for as long as she could afford to keep her eyes off the road. Which was pretty long, considering that Houston to Galveston was a fairly straight shot on a boring stretch of highway. "That's not really an answer. Is it classified? What country?" She let a smile slip to counter the sharpness of her tone, but the feeling that he was hedging irritated her.

"Austria." His head was turned away, but she could see no emotion on the reflection of his face in the tinted window of her Honda.

"You don't have an accent." No accent at all. Not anything from any of the American regions, and nothing foreign-sounding, either.

"I attended English-speaking private schools."

His sticking to the facts and lack of elaboration was discouraging. Keep asking or quit? Marissa traced the wheel with a fingertip. This wasn't looking like it would be a very eventful day. At this rate she was hesitant to ask about the headhunter thing.

"What about you? Where's your family from?"

Oh, now he was asking about her, when he wasn't willing to tell her jack about himself? Maybe he'd be more forthcoming if she opened up.

"Born and raised here." They crossed the final bridge into Galveston. "This is it. Galveston."

"I thought it would be bigger."

"No. It may have had a chance a hundred years ago,

before the big hurricane. Then things changed and it didn't become the hub it could have."

She turned into a Starbucks parking lot. "How about coffee and breakfast? We can enjoy it on the beach."

"I'll buy." He got out of the car.

He picked up coffees and an assortment of breakfast items to go, and then they were on their way to the beach.

She drove to the seawall and pulled into a parking place. "Let's do this."

"Do what?" He had a puzzled look on his face.

"It's an expression. Means, um—" Words escaped her. She'd never had to define things like this. "It just means let's go."

He opened the door and grabbed the food bags and coffee carrier. "Let's do this." His face lit up with a smile.

That's when it hit her. She hadn't seen that smile, that genuine grin on him as long as she'd known him.

Which isn't all that long.

Don't remind me.

She grabbed a couple of old towels from the back of her car and followed him down the stairs to the water. It was still early; most of the church-going families that would certainly later fill the sandy area weren't there yet. "It's going to get crowded. And hot," she warned him.

"We don't have to stay long. We can go hang out elsewhere if you like. But I'd like to finish our conversation from earlier."

Which part? she wondered. She'd rather finish the one where he answered some questions about himself, and not answer questions herself.

"And I don't just mean the stuff I asked."

"Don't worry, I wasn't going to let you get away with that."

Twelve steps and thirty feet of beachfront brown sand later, she was spreading the towels on the sand while he laid out the breakfast items.

She was surprised by the amount of food. "I think we have enough for lunch here, too. Maybe even dinner."

"I didn't know what you'd like, so I ordered one of everything."

A warmth built within her at his thoughtfulness. *Are you sure that's not hormones and lust at his hotness?* Could be a little bit of that, she had to admit.

He sat on the towel and pulled his shirt over his head, revealing a wide expanse of chest, no hair, tattoo of a winged—was that a woman?—on arms that belonged on a body builder. She fought to keep from staring, and turned her attention to a morning bun that wasn't one-tenth as appealing as his body.

"About you—" she started.

"I thought we could start with you." He sank his

teeth into a slice of banana bread with the ferocity of a large cat attacking prey, and a visual of his mouth sinking onto her, between her legs, this morning flashed through her mind.

"About a job…"

A weird look crossed his face. "Sure. But don't you have a job? Don't you own that restaurant?"

"Not exactly."

That question opened a floodgate. Before she knew it, she was filling him in on developers, an asshole banker, and a deadline she'd found out about yesterday. Then she revved up even more and started talking about her father. Hours went by, the food was half-eaten and the coffees half-drunk as well as lukewarm, since nothing got cold in the afternoon temperatures on the Gulf Coast, and she was drained—talked out and drained. She hadn't realized that sharing—blurting —that much out would be so tiring.

Sometime during their talk—which was mostly her monologue, as it turned out—Finn bought an umbrella from a man who was renting them out. Actually bought it, paying for its permanent use outright. He even told the guy he'd throw an extra twenty in if he brought them some bottled water, and, oh, the guy could keep the umbrella if they left the beach while he was still around. The guy shook his head and muttered something about some people having more money than sense, they said they could have just done a day rental and went off on a hunt for bottled water.

"I'm sorry for doing that, babbling so much. All you asked was about the restaurant."

He smiled, white teeth more pronounced against skin that was a shade more bronze. His eyes gleamed a darker blue than before, picking up the sky's brightness. Then it hit her, for the first time since she'd met him, which felt like it was ages ago, though it wasn't: his eyes didn't have a haunted look. He looked happy.

"I'm glad you shared with me."

"And I'm still waiting for you to share with me."

"I know. How about I do that over dinner?"

She hadn't thought that this would turn into a whole-day sort of thing, but she had to admit she'd enjoyed herself, more than she had in a long time. "What about your umbrella? You bought it, after all."

"Don't really need it. I'm sure someone else will enjoy it." He picked up the uneaten, now-hardened pastries and the coffee cups and dumped them in the trash barrel a few paces away.

She shouldn't have, but she couldn't help watching him walk away. To keep from getting caught, she turned just before he started back her way.

"How are you going to explain this, Marissa?" a voice asked.

Damn. Damn.

CHAPTER 26

One moment everything had seemed fine; they were having a great day, he was dumping the trash in the barrel, and the next moment some guy was snapping at Marissa, pointing a finger in her face.

Finn had noticed the guy walking up and down along the seawall behind them throughout the day, but had thought he was a random tourist or a local. But this guy knew Marissa's name and was threatening her. Finn double-timed it and got between them.

"You okay?" Keeping his eye on the newcomer, Finn didn't turn to look at Marissa.

"What the hell does that mean?" The man's face reddened between a haircut that was a shade too perfect and clothing that was too unrumpled. "Why would she not be okay? And who the hell are you?"

Finn eyed him, dismissed him as a non-threat.

"Who wants to know?"

"Her fiancé. That's who." The man sputtered his words out.

Finn hadn't seen any mention of a fiancé or even a boyfriend in the file, even though he was sure the files were up to date. "Marissa?" He glanced back at her.

Marissa put her hands on her hips and shook her head. "Ex. And not even fiancé. Finn, meet my cheating ex, Joey. And it's ex-boyfriend, not even ex-fiancé, by the way."

"Bullshit. Did she tell you I just proposed to her? That we went to her father's gravesite together? Did she? Two-timing whore."

"I forgot to mention delusional ex-boyfriend," Marissa added. "Oh, and I'd better not forget arrogant and self-centered."

"You bitch. After all I was willing to do for you." The man raised his arm.

Finn grabbed it and flipped him. The man landed with a thud, flat on his back.

It hadn't even registered to Finn that he was going to do it; he'd simply reacted. "Don't ever raise your hand to her again. Stay down." He put his hand on Marissa's lower back, guiding her. "Let's go."

The man, Joey, stayed in the sand.

Finn fought to regulate his breathing, to keep his wings from popping and his skin from changing. It took all his concentrated effort.

CHAPTER 27

*M*arissa didn't want to turn back to look at Joey, sprawled in the sand in an undignified position. "I can explain."

"You don't need to."

She couldn't tell if Finn was angry with her, believed Joey, or was simply indifferent to the whole thing.

"I want to. He's really my ex. Truly. He asked me to marry him in exchange for his funding the restaurant."

"I believe you." He was still expressionless.

"Why do I sense something?"

Then he turned her way with that same smile he'd given her earlier. "I'm fine. I believe you. He has nothing to do with us."

Us. She liked the sound of that, even though she

144

knew it didn't mean anything. He was a stranger from out of town who would probably be going back home again soon. "Okay."

Finn led her to a restaurant a little further down Seawall Boulevard. Luckily, Joey didn't follow.

Once they had a dinner of shrimp, rice pilaf, and sweet ice tea in front of them, Joey wasn't quite forgotten but wasn't at the forefront of Marissa's mind anymore.

Finn tore through his entrée and almost seemed to be eyeing hers.

"Want some of mine?" She thought it was polite to ask, though she didn't really want to share the delicious fare.

"I want some of you." His words drew a heat to her cheeks; she could feel a blush rising. His gaze saw right through to her own desire, barely kept at bay all day. She shimmied in her chair, squirming, trying to drive the yearning away.

Think. Think. Think. Something to say. Anything to keep from wanting to leave and get naked with this man. What was wrong with her? This wasn't her at all. "So where are you from?" Had those words really just popped out of her mouth? She'd asked that question before, and he'd answered it. She couldn't even control her train of thought, and her mouth went into autopilot.

A perplexed look crossed Finn's face. *He thinks* he's *confused.* He had no idea how she felt.

"I told you. Austria."

"Okay, is that all you're going to say about yourself? That you attended private schools, which explains why you don't have an accent? That's all I'm getting? After all that I told you?"

"You remind me of someone there."

Oh, great. An old girlfriend. Just what she needed. To remind a guy of an old girlfriend he'd never gotten over. Now she wished she hadn't asked. "I bet."

"My grandmother."

"Oh. I thought—" Now what? It had gone from bad to worse. Or had it? She'd gone from reminding him of an ex to reminding him of his grandmother. Very unsexy. "I'm not so sure that's a good thing. I'm sure she's not young."

"Actually, she's not alive." He took a long drink of the tea.

Now she felt like shit. "I'm sorry." What else was there to say?

"I meant to say, you remind me of what she was probably like when my grandfather met and fell in love with her. She was a—hu—American."

"That's romantic. Were you close to her?"

"She raised me. My mother died giving birth to me. Complications of some kind. My grandmother was brave. She moved to a fairly hostile land in the middle of a warzone, and made the most of a life with my grandfather. She risked a lot when she didn't have to."

This was the most he'd said to her in one sitting. Marissa didn't want to interrupt him by saying anything for fear he'd stop.

"Ready to go?" He put his napkin under his plate's lip and pushed back his chair.

"I guess you are?" She forced a laugh, saddened that he didn't want to contribute anything else. "Sure. That's okay."

Finn paid the tab, then suggested a walk.

The evening was balmy. A light breeze kept the humidity at bay and the ocean salt permeated the air.

Under a streetlamp, he stopped and pulled her to him.

"I want to thank you for today. It's probably one of the best days I've ever had." He leaned in and brushed her lips with his.

"Why does this sound like goodbye?" A sadness engulfed her.

He held her closer, his body hard against hers, his arms around her. The hug was tight, as if he didn't want to let her go, but knew he must. Tears threatened. Marissa didn't understand why it felt like goodbye, but what was far more alarming was the way that the blues overwhelmed her. She bit the tears back, forced the burning in her nose away. She wouldn't cry. No, she wouldn't. She forced herself to think. To speak, to change her train of thought and change the subject.

"Were you close to her?"

He paused. "My grandmother? Close enough. She was foreign. I had a hard time accepting her. Being related to her made me feel different."

Stay on track. Don't think about saying goodbye. "You mentioned she's not alive..."

"No. She died almost two weeks ago. I was out of town on a mission."

Alarms went off in her head. "Mission?"

"Yes, military."

She drew back and looked at his face. His eyes were deep, dark, indigo pools, his jaw strong and chiseled. The lips that had just touched hers were serious, somber.

"But I thought... didn't you say... aren't you a headhunter?"

"Maybe I'm not the kind of headhunter you think I am."

Chills made their way across her flesh, and she fought the urge to push away. "You're freaking me out now." She rubbed her arms to scrub the goosebumps away. "I don't know what that's supposed to mean. Should I be afraid of you?"

"Never."

And somehow she felt she could believe that one word. "Then you have some explaining to do."

A blow to her back that felt like a brick wall knocked the breath and the words out of her.

A hoodie-shadowed face was next to hers. The tip of a knife pricked at her neck.

"Your wallet, bitch," a gravelly voice said next to her ear.

"Now," another voice demanded, this one higher-pitched. In the background a third figure was silent.

"Let her go." Finn's voice was different. Almost scary.

It was a blur, everything moved so fast.

Finn catapulted forward.

The guy holding her dropped, without uttering a sound.

The other guy pounced closer. The third one was immobile.

A flash of steel near Finn.

He grunted, dropped to one knee, rose, and was almost a blur again.

The second man fell. Both men stayed down. The third one ran, but not before his hood had fallen off, revealing Joey's profile just before he turned and sprinted away.

"Joey." The word escaped from her lips. "That was him."

"It sure was. Doesn't matter, he's gone. I'll take care of him later." Finn touched her neck. "I want to be sure you're all right. Are you?"

"Yes. Are you? I thought they got you when you fell."

"I'm good. They—"

He stumbled and fell between the two men on the concrete.

CHAPTER 28

The second man had gotten him. There was a slice on Finn's arm, another on his thigh. Blood warmed him, and his clothing stuck to the wetness.

Marissa put a hand on his arm, then jerked it back. "You're bleeding."

He put weight on one leg, not the one with the cut, then pushed himself up. "I'm fine." His knee buckled, and he almost fell, catching himself on the thigh-high seawall. "I need to rest."

"We need to get the cops."

"No police."

"Why the hell not?" She put both hands on her hips.

He would have smiled if he weren't in so much cursed pain. "No police. Can we go, please?"

She grumbled, but led him toward her car. He was getting weaker with each step. "You saved my life."

"It's nothing." He heaved the car door open. It felt fifty times heavier than the last time he'd opened it. He was getting weaker.

She buckled herself in. "Now what?"

"Rest. Somewhere to recoup."

"You need a doctor."

"No. Just take me somewhere private."

"No doctor. No police. What gives?"

"It's complicated."

"Simplify it."

"I'm—" His mind raced. What could he say? He couldn't get words to turn into thoughts. "I'm AWOL."

"Does it have something to do with your grandmother?"

He latched onto the lie. "Pretty much." His wings pressed against the skin in his back. He was converting. He had to stop the process, and if he couldn't, he needed to be alone. "I need somewhere." He leaned the seat back.

"I'll get a hotel room."

He didn't know how much time had lapsed when he felt the car come to a stop. He opened his eyes. They were in a hotel parking lot.

"Be right back." Marissa pushed her door open.

"Please, no medics or police."

With a shake of her head, she closed the door.

He was at her mercy. A position Finn didn't like being in, at someone else's mercy.

CHAPTER 29

Marissa helped Finn into the room. He leaned against her, his weight heavy until they reached the bed, then he collapsed onto it, an undignified heap.

Marissa stretched him out, took a sheet off the second bed and nicked it with her fingernail clippers, then ripped it into strips. She couldn't see the wound on his leg well enough to access it so she unbuckled his pants and began the slow process of taking them off his long body. She couldn't allow it to take too long; the amount of blood was alarming.

Once his pants were off, she held a washcloth to the sliced flesh with one hand and tried to weave the strip of sheet under his thigh and around to the other side so she could tourniquet it, cursing under her breath the entire time. The stupid man wouldn't let her take him to a hospital. Ignorant!

She studied the wounds. Then she rubbed her eyes. She was seeing things. She rubbed them again. No, his skin, it looked... green. Then it looked like a light fluorescent blue. She was tired, hallucinating. Three paces later she was in front of the bathroom sink, splashing her face with cold water.

Behind her, Finn moaned. She turned around, dropped the towel, and backed up a pace.

"Holy shit." Her retreat was halted by the countertop behind her.

Finn's color had changed again. Now it was a bright, shifting green. It looked like the brightest chameleon's skin, rippling under the surface with luminous shades of emerald.

Finn was mumbling something under his breath. She wanted to go closer, but fear froze her feet to the carpeting.

"Marissa. Must save Marissa." His voice was audible now, the words clear.

His skin changed color again, becoming a wave of undulating tangerine hues, shifting from his face, down his chest, over his abdomen.

What the hell was going on here? She looked at her purse, lying on the dresser across the room. She could grab it and her keys and leave. Never see him again. Except he knew where she lived.

What was he? She stepped toward the end of the bed, one pace closer to her purse.

His mouth opened again. "Marissa. Can't let her get hurt." His eyes were still closed.

Did he know what he was saying? More importantly, what *was* he saying? What did he mean? Save her from what? Couldn't let what hurt her? Was he reliving the attempted mugging?

So you're going to leave this man who just saved your life?

She rubbed her temples and took a step closer to her purse, keeping her eyes on Finn.

Wait a moment. The man who'd saved her life? Man? Who said this was a man? He wasn't like any man she'd ever met before. This changing-skin thing... that couldn't be good.

She was torn. Half of her wanted to get the hell out of there. The other half felt like she owed this injured man—being—thing—whatever he was—

She owed him something.

When he sat up, she thought he was reaching for her. She sidestepped to the right, closer to the mirror and the television. His eyes were still closed, and his skin was still doing that undulating thing and shifting colors. His moans were low, and he didn't say anything else.

"Finn?" She kept her voice to a whisper. She didn't really want to wake him if he wasn't awake, but she also didn't want to walk past him if he was awake and pissed that she was trying to escape.

Are you really trying to escape? Damn her inner voice. She didn't need the pressure.

She took a couple of steps closer to the door. She was almost in front of him. He was still moaning, but now he shifted slightly.

Suddenly he bolted upright to a sitting position. His eyes were still closed. Behind him something moved, then there was a fluttering sound, almost imperceptible.

Marissa jumped back.

He had wings.

Or something like wings. No, no, no. It was definitely wings. They had spread out, a pair of white, almost opaque things—wings—whatever.

Making sure his eyes were still closed, she leaned in for a better look. Those wings looked like a diaphanous fabric.

This couldn't be. How could she have missed that? What the hell was he? Why was she still here?

That did it. She needed to be out of here. Gone. Done. Over it already.

She glanced at the door, then back at him. Curiosity was getting the best of her, but mostly because she'd always felt so safe around him. She let a breath out she hadn't realized she was holding.

Maybe he was a demon. Or an angel. Screw this, she

was out of here. There was no reason to find out what he was. This wasn't something she wanted to be involved in, whatever it was. Whatever he was. She clutched her purse to her chest and tiptoed toward the door.

She didn't get two steps before a hoarse whisper called her name.

Finn's voice was tortured. Great. Just what she needed. Because she was a sucker.

"Where are you going?"

Disbelief froze her feet. "You ask me that when you have those—those—wings? Or whatever those things are."

He shrugged, but it was more like a shrug to figure out if something was there. As if to determine that the wings were there, not as if to say 'I don't know.'

He nodded. "That's what they are."

She folded her arms over her chest. Was this guy for real? Jeez, was he even a guy? Not as in male ... her mind didn't want to go there because he was definitely all male, but more like, was he even human? "How can you be so nonchalant?"

Oh, boy, she was getting more and more pissed by the moment. She fought the urge to stomp around the end of the bed. Or maybe to throw something. "And what world do you live in that you don't think you should tell a girl—ugh!—" She didn't want to say it out

loud. What else could she say, though? "We did *things!*
Naked *things*—and—are you even human?"

"A quarter."

His wings folded back. Or he folded them back.
Who the hell knew at this point? She sure didn't.
"What? Quarter... what? What are you talking about?"
She had to struggle to keep her hysteria from making
her voice rise. She wondered if she should be scared.
But this was Finn. She couldn't fear him. There was
something innate about the trust she felt around him.
But right now, her anger was overriding all other
emotions. "Well? What?"

"I'm a quarter human." His voice was calm, his
words enunciated clearly, as if he was talking to a dull-
witted person. "Three quarters Asazi. My grandmother. She was human."

"So she's real? Because I was starting to wonder if
anything you've told me is the truth."

"She was very real."

"So you're only a quarter human and three
quarters...?"

"Asazi."

"Which is what? And from where?"

"It's a long story."

"I've got time."

"You look like you're leaving."

"Let's see. A guy I was *sexual* with sprouted wings
and has skin that's a cross between a dragon and a

chameleon. You're not seriously asking why I'd consider leaving, are you?"

He looked down. "I guess not."

"So what's your story? And make it the short version. I get bored easily."

She wondered if she was being too bitchy. Nah, he—he'd lied. Or at the very least, he'd misrepresented himself. Then again, another part of her asked, *What was he supposed to say? Don't freak out, but I have wings and this cool skin that ripples different colors?* Like he would have said that? Like she would have believed it?

She uncrossed her arms and leaned back against the dresser, trying hard not to look as pissed and confused as she felt.

"Short version. I'm from another planet. We used to live on Earth, but were banished. We came to get resources. Our wings don't work." He stopped, bit down on his lip, then released it and stared at her. As if he were waiting. As if it were up to her. As if anything were up to her.

She sucked air in, then heaved a breath out. "Maybe I shouldn't have asked for the short version."

His face was somber, open, and vulnerable. A look she'd never seen on him before.

"Do you trust me?" His voice was just as somber, open, and vulnerable.

She didn't pause to think. If she were to spend any time thinking of the answer to that one, she wasn't sure she would be completely honest. So she dove right in. "That's a strange question. But my answer may be stranger, because I don't think I understand it completely. I trust you not to bring me physical harm."

A question was forming in his expression, a brief frown. "As opposed to?"

"Lying to me, Mr. Headhunter." She hoped that her statement stung as much as the lies he'd told her did, or as much as the truths he hadn't revealed stung.

His color shifted to a bluish shimmer.

"Wait. Wait a damned moment. Why did your color just change?"

"It matches our emotions. We cannot lie in our own skin. It's different in human skin. That masks our emotions."

She had to know, because for some stupid reason she had begun to feel *something* for him. "How do you become human?"

"Adjust our heart rate, then draw our skin over our wings and transform our skin's appearance by adding a human layer."

"So, are you in your true form right now? Not some in-between form? I mean, because except for the wings and the color-changing thing, you look very human." She didn't add, *very hot and sexy and very human*. Some things shouldn't be said, especially not at a time like this. "And you said your wings don't work? Meaning you can't fly?"

"Yes, this is my true Asazi form. And that is correct. We haven't been able to fly since the Banishment."

"Banishment—what?"

His smile was rueful. "I told you it was a long story. You said you wanted the shortened version."

"Wait. What happened to your wounds?" She approached, reached for his leg, put her hand on it. The wound had healed. "What the hell is going on here?"

"We heal fast."

"We is who?"

"Asazi people."

"You say people, but people don't have wings, don't do that skin color thing. And people live on Earth. Why are you on Earth, again?"

"We're having problems with procreation."

A blush warmed her cheeks as she thought of his body. "What do you mean, you can't procreate? You have the equipment. And you didn't look like you have problems to me."

"Our females."

"Have you people thought of e-mail brides?"

"We need something. I'm not sure what. I'm a soldier, not a scientist. I deliver the females."

"And I'm one of them."

"You were. Now I'm..." He hesitated.

She wondered what he was going to say. "So your grandmother dying is bullshit? Is she even human? Not that I believe any of this, but shit, you have wings. So I guess something's true. Maybe you're an angel."

"My grandmother. That's not bullshit. And she really died. And she's human. And I'm part human."

"And my meeting you really wasn't an accident. You really are hunting me?"

"Not hunting. But you aren't an accident. You were my first target."

"I am?"

"No. I rearranged the order."

"You're allowed to do that? Why did you do that?"

"No. And I don't know. There's something about you. So I picked up 42. Kal said she was brought home after they were done with her. But she wasn't. She's missing. They ordered me to return to the ship. But I didn't go. I left. I ran away. And then you."

"Me. Yeah. Me. Drunk me in the bar. Easy pickings."

Marissa's touch on his thigh, near the almost-healed wound, felt like his flesh was on fire. Not from pain, but from desire. The need to have her touch him radiated from her fingertips to his loins, traveling, searing his entire body. Finn rubbed his head. "I'm confused. My body's been acting —feeling—strange, different. My mind too. Everything seems off sometimes. Makes me wonder why. Maybe it's the human food."

"How can that be?"

"Not sure. I'm a soldier. Not a scientist."

"Now I'm the one who's confused."

He took her hand in his, bringing her nearer. Her face showed the conflict she felt at his betrayal. And it showed something else. He wasn't sure he could diagnose it, but—

He pulled her even closer. At first she resisted, holding back, but he didn't relinquish his hold.

When she was leaning over him, he took her other hand in his and settled her next to him on the bed. Her leg was lined up with his, his bare thigh against hers. His skin was aware of her body heat like nothing he'd ever felt before, and his breathing became shallower.

He raised his eyes from their legs and looked into hers. Her pupils dilated, then contracted. She cleared her throat in a way that he'd already become familiar with. She licked her bottom lip, driving him over the edge—almost.

"Finn." Her voice was throaty, lingering on every nerve in his body, pressing him with the need to have her. "I'm confused. And I know I should be worried, pissed, frustrated, betrayed—I should feel all those things, but I can't—I don't."

"I never meant to hurt you. If I could have avoided deceiving you, I would have. If I could have stopped you from thinking I was something I'm not, I would have."

"I know. But where does that leave us now?"

He pressed his lips against hers, inhaling her scent. All woman. All human. His tongue touched her bottom lip. She moaned, and his shaft filled with need, pressing against his briefs. She'd see it. Then she'd think—

She was more confused than he was. Or was she? This beautiful man with dark, predatory eyes and *wings—jeez, don't fucking forget the wings!*—was on this bed in a very—

She avoided looking down at his state of arousal again. Avoided it, because it made her want him so much more. And she didn't want to want him. She didn't understand wanting him. Was it okay that he had lied to her? Was it self-preservation? It didn't feel the way it did when Joey lied. Not at all.

Finn's face was honest, his eyes clear, and it was obvious it pained him to lie to her.

"What are we doing?" She couldn't keep the whisper back, though she wasn't sure she wanted to know the answer to that. If she could handle the answer.

He put a finger on the button on her shirt, then

under it, slipping beneath the fabric. His fingertip brushed her skin lightly, nothing more than a graze, sending a typhoon of sensations throughout her body. Her breath was held hostage in her lungs, burning now, while she waited for his next move.

He unbuttoned a button, then two fingers slipped into her blouse, then another. He raised his hand and almost delicately traced the contour of her breast. Her nipple pressed against the fabric, seeking freedom from its satin casing, seeking the warmth and roughness of his hands. Confusion battled desire. Anger and frustration no longer factored into the equation.

"I don't want to do something you don't want." His breath was warm on her cheek.

What she wanted was to feel every inch of him on and in every bit of her. But what she needed to do was run away from this man who wasn't even human. Who was much more than human. A being she didn't understand.

"How can you seem so real, and yet be so surreal?" Her thoughts flowed from her mind to her lips. She couldn't have stopped saying that if she'd wanted to.

"How can you?" He unbuttoned the next button, never taking his eyes off her face. Then he moved to another and another. The room's air flow cooled her flesh. Marissa closed her eyes as he pushed her top off her shoulders. She fought to control the pure yearning that flowed through her nerves, her blood, her tendons, and coursed throughout her body.

"Look at me." His voice brooked no hesitation.

She opened her eyes. His face had a faint greenish hue that alternated with a purple shade.

"Do you want me to convert? I can make my skin human and the wings can completely vanish."

Good grief. She'd forgotten about his wings. One minute they were there, stretched out and now, they weren't. "What did you do with them?"

"Nothing. They're furled. You know, wrapped up."

"I want to touch them."

He picked her up and shifted her onto his lap so she was facing him. He put his hands over hers, raised them and put them on his shoulders. "Touch them."

She ran her fingers over his tense shoulder muscles, their bulging mass a reminder of his maleness. She encountered resistance at the points of his shoulder blades, bone covered with what felt like the softest of fabrics. "They don't even feel like skin. They aren't feathered."

Finn's laugh was soft and gentle. "No. We aren't birds, you know." His hands were on her shoulders, tracing tiny circles that expanded as he lowered them down her back to her bra. With the slightest hint of a struggle he unclasped the bra and slid it down. She shrugged it off, then put her hands on his shoulders again. He pulled her close, her breasts pressed against his naked flesh.

Against her sex, his shaft was hard, insistent.

Marissa shifted, pushing her sundress away, his hardness pressed against her folds, separated from her only by the sheer pink panties she'd put on this morning. Damp panties, a testament to the desire she felt for him.

He moved his hips, pressing his shaft against her clit, back and forth. The gasp she made didn't even sound like her own voice.

"Finn."

Marissa leaned to the side, reached under the leg band of her panties and shoved them out of the way. She rose on her knees, then lowered herself until the tip of him was pressing against her entrance.

Finn placed his hands on her hips. Lifting his body, he entered her the slightest bit, his eyes closed and a low groan escaping his lips.

Marissa breathed out, waiting, hoping, feeling his heat pressing, promising against her lust-slick folds.

With a sudden burst he drew her onto him, filling her, expanding her, completing her. Every bit of her was full, almost painfully so.

"Damn." Her words were uttered, barely.

"Are you okay?" He rocked her back and forth, then raised and lowered her on his shaft, her juices making sloppy noises that turned her on even more.

She couldn't answer him; she didn't trust her voice. She nodded and ground on him, taking him in deeper, enjoying the pain that suffused the pleasure.

He leaned against the headboard while she rocked on him, and she reached between her folds, touching her clit, rubbing it, each touch making the next one more frantic.

When Finn joined his fingers with hers, spreading her open, watching what she was doing, then doing what she did, she slammed herself onto him, time after time, her wetness increasing, and her tempo wild. A release was building up like a tidal wave. She leaned back, hoping to postpone it, not wanting to yield to the overwhelming sensations that threatened to send her out of control. "Stop, god, stop."

Instead of stopping, Finn put an arm around her and turned her over. She watched in the mirror, his face a vision of lust, sexiness, and intensity—and all of it with a tinge of colors that drifted from green to a light purple.

Behind her he spread her legs, put his forearm under her and raised her up and backward. He pushed her legs apart, and she raised her hips, ready, wanting.

Finn drove into her with a grunt that paralleled her own at the sensation of being filled.

He pumped her body mercilessly, each pump bringing her closer and closer to the same tidal pool that had threatened her earlier.

"Stop holding back. I want to see you as you are. As you can be," Finn demanded.

With his words, his glorious wings expanded behind him.

A surge like an electric current flowed through her, and a scream followed in its wake as shudders and spasms shook her body. Her back arched, then she pushed against him, taking more of him into her pulsing, contracting muscles.

With a cry and a grimace on his sexy face, his expression one of pure ecstasy, he pulled her tight against him, filling her. Pressure pushed against her as he came undone inside her.

She collapsed on the bed, still wracked with an occasional spasm.

He lay next to her, touching her skin, running his fingers over her back. "I never would have imagined that was what it would be like." His voice was breathless, exerted, exhausted. "So much lost control."

"I've never felt anything that intense. Wait. What do you mean? You mean you didn't imagine that's what it would be like with a human?"

"With anyone. Asazi don't do that—this—it." His fingers traveled lower, over the curve of her bottom, toward her thigh.

"Ever? Then how'd you know what to do?"

His fingers went lower, between her legs, swirling

through the juices they'd made. "There was a video, at my hotel."

"That's called porn. It's not quite like the real thing."

"I'm convinced of that."

"How do your women get pregnant, if you don't—you know..."

"Our children are planned, and it depends on the—"

When he stopped, she knew what he was going to say, and didn't want to say. The reason he'd met her. The reason he was here. What he had to do with her.

"So what's your plan? For me? For you?"

"I have not fully formulated one. One thing I am certain of, is that I don't plan to return. I don't think I can."

"You can stay with me."

Had those words just come out of her mouth? Marissa wanted to bite her tongue. What the hell was she thinking? She had no job, and who knew what was up with him.

"My concern is that they will come for you."

"I'm not safe? My house isn't? Surely they can't find me."

"I don't think you're safe."

"Because I'm a target. But you don't know why? Really? And you have no idea? Not even a guess?"

"If I had to guess—I'd say they want your eggs, or genes, or something."

What the hell. She sat upright. "So what's your role in all of this? And why would you agree to do it?"

"I'm a soldier. It's not optional. I'm supposed to bring you in."

"And?"

"It doesn't look like I will."

"Why not?"

He rubbed his head. "I'm not sure."

"Now what?"

"My career will be gone. I would probably be tried for treason if I return. I could end up in prison."

She paused a moment, taking it all in. "All for me."

"It seemed the right thing to do."

She was curious about so much. She didn't know where to start. "Why don't your people relocate? Come back to Earth?"

He kissed the tip of her nose, his face a tint of green. "Could you move all of Earth's population, all of them, today?"

Marissa pondered his question. It seemed silly at first, but she was starting to see where he was going. "No, we don't have enough transportation, rockets, whatever."

"Exactly. There may not be as many of us, but we still don't have the means."

"How did you leave Earth if this was long ago?"

"I don't know. The Sacred Writings say we were moved during the Banishment. The writings are not exact. It's like they speak in riddles at times. Our wings were rendered useless after our people broke certain tenets. We were banished to the place we live now."

"So you have a god?"

"One I'm not really sure I believe in, to be honest."

"And that tattoo?" She pointed to his arm.

"It's an Asazi legend."

"A woman? Who's winged?"

He nodded. "Her child is to be the one who takes us home."

"And Earth is home." She nodded. "Interesting story."

"That's why I said, I'm not sure anymore what I believe in. I believe in things I can touch, things I know. I know I'm here. I know I have feelings for you. I know I can survive without Asazi food though I was led to believe I can't. I know that I'm more human than I thought I was. I'm not sure about the rest of our people, and to what degree. They weren't born of humans. Once, long ago, they were—some of them were."

"But they look like you? You really could pass for one of us, minus the wings and the colorful skin. And the place you live now? Tell me about Asazi."

"Asazi are my people. We live on Kormia. Its natives are called the Kormic. Kormia is beautiful, but full of danger, because of the Kormic. They will not rest until we are extinct, or dominated fully."

This information was overwhelming, too much to digest. Now what? She waited for more, but he gave her nothing. They were both silent.

Car doors closed outside. Finn jumped to his feet. Pulling aside the drapes, he looked out the window. When he spoke, his voice was low. "Curses. They're here. They're going to the front office. Let's go."

She wanted to ask who was there, but she didn't have a chance. He'd grabbed their clothes and her bag and they were in front of the door. Completely nude. Something in her wanted to react. Wanted to protest. But the urgency in his tone and manner corked all of her responses. If he thought it was that important, she wasn't going to argue, not when it seemed that his mission was her safety.

He opened the door slowly, and soundlessly, they slipped onto the veranda, then she saw what he was looking at. A car, and a man next to it. Two other men were bound for the registration desk.

Finn led her the other way, still holding her hand in one of his and their things in the other.

They rounded the corner and slid down the outdoor metal stairs with stealth, hidden by the ice machine. Two more floors to go.

Her nudity bugged her, despite the direness of the situation. "Finn, can I get dressed, please?"

He froze, looking down. He clamped a hand over her face.

Marissa glanced in the same direction. A man was at the base of the stairs, looking the other away.

"Your wings." Translucent webs extended behind him. The wings flapped, fanning her with air. "Unbelievable. And they don't work? At all?" she mumbled under his hand, peeling his fingers away.

"No. Asazi wings don't work. We cannot fly."

"Um, then, why are your feet not touching the ground?"

He looked down. "Curses." But he kept rising. "Curses. I can fly. I can. I'm not even sure how I'm controlling this—these—it." He dropped to the floor and enveloped her in his arms. "Come here."

She wanted to say, *Hell, no.* But she wrapped her arms around his neck.

CHAPTER 32

Finn didn't have time to process this miracle. Not with Asazi soldiers a few yards away. He flew up, and up, and up. He wanted to laugh with joy at this amazing development. The first thought he had was how much this would help the Asazi in a battle with the Kormic. But he had more pressing issues to tend to, like saving Marissa, so he had to let that thought go. For now.

North. He knew that Houston was north of Galveston. And right now he needed to be able to hide amongst the human population. So he flew north.

In a short time he could see the city lights of Houston glowing in the distance. He made for the highest point with the least amount of light and alit on the rooftop of a high-rise in downtown Houston, overlooking the bustling, traffic-laden metropolis. He handed Marissa her clothes, though he'd enjoyed her body pressing against his for the flight.

She slipped behind a large metal box. He heard the rustling of clothing as she dressed.

"Now what?" she asked.

"I'm not sure. Things are confusing. My wings aren't supposed to work. They never have. No Asazi has functioning wings. And earlier, when your fiancé and those guys attacked—I don't move that fast. I never have."

"Ex!" She emerged, folding her arms over her chest, angry. A beautiful, fierce vision, hair askew, eyes on fire with green light. "So what do you think? What's different? Why do you have these... superpowers? Being on Earth? Being part human?"

He needed to think. And he didn't want to voice his suspicions yet. They were too uncertain.

"So tell me more about where you're from. And how you were on Earth before."

He wanted to tell her the answers to her questions even less than he wanted to tell her about his suspicions as to why he could fly, or move so fast. But he owed her something. The least he could deliver was answers.

"Originally we lived on your world, among humans, occasionally interacting. Long ago we were banished. Sent to another world, one inhabited by others. We battled, we lost. My people, the Asazi, live in hiding from the Kormic. We have battles at times. We're working to return to Earth to claim our lands. Some of our buildings still exist, here—on Earth. Earth's people have no idea about us, only theories and speculation."

"Why don't you leave that other planet? If it's so bad, I mean."

"As I said, it's not easy to move an entire population."

"And Asazi are harvesting our eggs?"

"I can't be sure that's what our scientists are doing, but it's the best I can come up with."

"Why don't the Asazi try harvesting Kormic eggs? Instead of traveling to the far ends of the galaxy?"

"It's been tried, with captive Kormic. The results were disastrous."

He paced up and down the roof of the high-rise. What could he do now? Who would help her? How could he leave her? Could he? Should he hide her and return to the ship and be a failure at his mission, but know that she was safe? What if his people scheduled another Wave? Would she be targeted? Would she ever be safe?

He wished he could talk to Kal, unsupervised, uncensored. Ask him if he thought there was a way to leave Marissa out of the mission.

He would go back to the ship, then wait and see if he had a chance for some privacy with Kal. If he was found, he'd claim he couldn't find her. Would they know different?

They'd been at the hotel. Who were they following? Him or her? Him, probably. A thought came to mind. He took the phone out of his pocket and placed it in a crevice on the high rise-rooftop. He'd have to keep moving if this was how they'd found him. If they'd used the phone to track him.

He turned back to look at the woman, the vision—chest heaving, this dark-haired, curvy hellion. A woman who had become much more to him than he'd thought possible.

He sucked a deep breath in, knowing that his next step would be difficult. "I have to go."

CHAPTER 33

"Bullshit." Marissa stormed over to him. This man, this being, this beautiful image from another place that she was figuring out she didn't want gone from her life. "You're not going anywhere. You drop all these info-bombs on me. You leave my car in Galveston. I'm here in Houston, people are hunting me to do things to me—surgical shit. And you say you're leaving?" She grabbed his arm, the hardness flexing beneath her fingertips. "Bullshit." She looked into his eyes, seeing the pain in them as his face tinged with blue.

"I just want to go look for my people. To see if they've left. To see what's going on. To see if you're safe."

She huffed. Men. Half-men. Whatever. "You just don't get it, do you?"

"I think you'd be safer up here, than if you were with me."

"I'd be trapped up here. At least you could fly me away if there was danger."

"Listen," he started.

She put two fingers over his lips and slid her other hand up his arm, over his shoulder, behind his neck, and pulled his face to hers. "Finn. Please." His breath was warm against her mouth. She kissed his lower lip, sucked on it gently, traced it with her tongue.

"You're making things happen." His voice was hoarse, sexy.

"They've already happened." She didn't want to expand on that. How could she possibly explain to him that there were these feelings for him—strong ones— deep within her?

"Let me go check for you. I won't bother you again after that if you don't want me to. I'll stay away."

Disbelief flooded throughout her body. Did he still not get it? What did he think she'd meant by what she'd just said? "Finn, I don't want you to leave."

He leaned back and took her face in his hands, cupping her jaw, his gaze boring into her eyes, reaching her soul. His own expression was confused. "After everything—"

She shook her head. "I don't get it either. I don't want you to go, though." She stepped back, hands on her hips. "And I sure as hell don't want you to leave me here." And yet she didn't want to go close to the ship. Couldn't they just run away somewhere?

The logical part of her brain laughed at her ignorance. *He's not even an American citizen. He can't hold a job. You'll be losing your job in a matter of days. And you have no prospects.*

Marissa rubbed up and down her arms, even though it wasn't cold.

"What is it?" Finn tugged her top, pulling her back into his arms.

"I'm worried. You can't go. We shouldn't go. But we will. Then what? What will happen?"

"Don't worry. I'll fly us there. We'll stay in a grove of trees nearby. They won't see us. We'll see what's going on and then we'll go."

"And then?"

"We'll make a plan. I'm not sure what that is yet, but at least let's make sure my people go so you're not under threat." A smile lit up his face, but the frown that lined his forehead didn't go completely away. "Ready?" He held his arms out.

She shivered, not sure if it was from the breeze that had picked up or something else.

CHAPTER 34

Finn inhaled as much air as he could, filling his lungs, his chest. "Ready?" He tried to infuse confidence in his words, but he couldn't even convince himself. What if he couldn't fly again? What had allowed him to fly the first time? What if he took off from the roof and they plummeted to their deaths? So much for saving her.

"What's wrong?" Marissa looked up, pushing her hair back from her face.

Her laser-sharp gaze saw right through him. He was convinced of that. Should he tell her? That wouldn't solve anything.

"Nothing. Just checking the wind. Thinking things through." His best bet would be to start the flying thing at the end of the building. That way, if they fell, they'd fall on the rooftop, making it serve as his landing strip, rather than crashing dozens of floors down, onto the concrete Houston sidewalks.

He took her hand and led her to the other end of the roof. "We'll start here."

"You're worried."

Damnation. She knew him too well.

"You're worried it won't work."

"It's still a foreign skill for me. I can't say I'm used to it yet."

"Finn. You can do this. You did it before."

He'd been full of adrenaline and worried when he did it before. What if it didn't work now? What if he couldn't figure it out? "Let me do a test run first, just to be sure."

"No way. You'll leave me. You'll go off on your own like you planned to do. Not a chance." She hunched over, poised like a runner. "I'll catch you if you try to fly off."

He couldn't help the laugh that exploded from his body. And it felt good. He'd never laughed so hard before. This sweet, tender woman was threatening to tackle him, and at the same time, she was the tigress who'd been in his bed earlier. He took her chin in his hand. "I won't leave you. I promise on all that is holy. On all that I believe in."

"You said you don't believe in much."

"I swear it. On my grandmother."

"You test your wings. I'll wait." Her jaw's set was determined, and her eyes were green flint in the semi-darkness. "Don't go far, Finn."

CHAPTER 35

Finn took a few steps back, his face appearing cast in stone, resolute. Because he was wearing only a pair of jeans, his wings spread behind him, and he rose straight up, the air pushed by his flight fanning Marissa's face. She bit back the giddy laughter that threatened to come out. She didn't want him to know she'd been worried too. Worried that he'd crash-dive both of them into the ground below.

He made a slow spin around the rooftop, and her eyes stayed on him as he circled above her. She rotated with his motions, then—

Oh, god.

No.

He was gone from sight. Vanished. He'd plunged like a stone.

The same boulder dropped in Marissa's stomach.

No, this couldn't be happening. She rushed to the end of the building, her lungs burning from exertion and fear.

She drew to a quick stop at the end of the building. She didn't want to look over the side. She couldn't bear the thought of seeing Finn's body lying on the sidewalk, blood pouring out of him while a crowd grew around him, fascinated by the man with wings.

She dropped to her knees, then sat against the brick wall, her head in her hands. Hot tears coursed down her cheeks. She could still smell him on her body, and now he was gone. Forever. Her hero, her savior.

"I'm sorry, Finn." Her tears turned to sobs.

A soft breeze fanned her hair. How could the world still be functioning, the traffic zooming, honking, the wind blowing, the moon beaming its faint glow, while down below an amazing man lay dead, just waiting to attract attention, to be featured on the news?

"What are you sorry for?"

Finn's voice.

Finn!

Marissa raised her head. He was right above her, creating the breeze with his wings, his skin a beautiful green tint. She jumped to her feet, grabbed his legs and pulled him down.

"Don't you ever scare me like that again. I thought —I—it looked like..." She wiped her tears away with impatient hands.

"I didn't do anything. I was testing my wings."

"It looked like you were falling. Like you lost control."

With one fingertip beneath her chin, he raised her face, studying her. "You were crying for me? You were worried?"

"That's hard to believe?" It almost seemed as though this was a foreign concept to him. Marissa struggled to remember that he wasn't like her. But she couldn't figure out what he *was* like. Did he not have emotions? If he didn't, then why had he saved her?

"No." A perplexed expression flashed over his features. "Ready?" He held his arms out.

She had so many questions to ask him, but this didn't seem like the right time. Would there ever be a right time? A chance? A reason to ask him about the Asazi and his emotions?

She let him wrap his arms around her, then put her hands on his neck and turned her face into his bare chest, so that his wings weren't encumbered. It struck her how commonplace it was now for her to see his colors changing and his wings there behind him.

She took a deep breath, inhaling his scent and the scent they'd created together. "Ready," she whispered, so he couldn't hear her. She was ready for whatever. Her adrenaline dropped, fatigue set in, and she nuzzled against his body.

◦∼◦

MARISSA STARTLED AWAKE. Something was different. She was still in Finn's arms. She pulled her face away from his warm chest, away from the strong heartbeat. They were on the ground. Unsure of the level of danger, she kept her voice to a whisper. "Where are we?" Through the night's darkness, she could see the silhouettes of pines and oak trees surrounding them. Scrub and brush locked out most of the moon's faint light.

"In a thicket near the compound. I can see the entrance. I want to see who's coming and going. If they look like they're ready to go back. And what kind of threat they may pose."

"What sort of compound is this?"

"It's an underground one, on land our people own. We've owned the land for a long time. We own several properties scattered around the world. Have bank accounts. We're preparing for our eventual Ultimate Passage."

The chirp of crickets punctuated Finn's explanation.

"So you do have a way to move to Earth? You could do it today if you had the transportation?"

"We don't have the transport, anyway. But I believe that an influx that large wouldn't go unnoticed, even if it was spread out over several countries."

"What language do you speak, where you're from?"

"Asazi. But we are all trained in English. Though we don't use it except when we have to. Well, I did." He shrugged. "My grandmother was American, and she felt more comfortable with that language."

"She wanted to be with your people?"

"She loved my grandfather. And he felt the same way." His skin glowed a blue tinge in the dimness. She had come to recognize that as sadness. Unless it had other emotions tied to it. She'd have to ask him sometime. "You don't like emotions, do you? Are all your people that way?"

"Yes. It's what separates us from baser creatures. Humans, animals."

Marissa fought her anger at that revelation. "Baser? You're comparing us to animals?"

"That's not how I feel. That's—" He visibly struggled for words, for an explanation, and a flash of orange flowed over his face and neck, then subsided. "How some think. Not all."

A wave of sadness poured through her. "Was your grandmother happy?"

"I think so. She never said she regretted leaving Earth. She never asked to return."

"That—"

Finn put a finger over her lips, then pointed.

Headlights were approaching from a distance.

CHAPTER 36

Finn had shared with her the information Kal had given him before they left their home. He knew Kal hadn't told him everything he knew, but he also wasn't convinced that Kal knew everything there was to know. He wasn't that high a rank. And even though he was a Governor-Select, that didn't mean that Finn's uncle would share everything with his son Kal.

He knew she'd gotten upset. He knew that she wouldn't understand some Asazi ways. He wasn't sure he understood them himself.

He waited for the car to approach. He didn't recognize the vehicle, but then again none of them had shared what vehicles they'd rented. The car came to a halt, and the engine was killed.

Merck emerged from the driver's side, rounded the

car and opened the passenger door. He reached in and came out with a woman.

Marissa gasped. Finn clamped his hand over her mouth.

They couldn't afford to be found, not in this thicket, not where he had no way to lift off and fly away. He cursed himself for deciding to hide here. Cover would mean nothing if they were heard and if he needed to make a quick escape.

Behind him, a crunch signaled a footfall. He whirled around, pushing Marissa behind him.

Blinding lights shone in his eyes.

"Lieutenant Ramont," a voice said in Asazi.

He needed to think, quick and now and—

Finn saluted. "Reporting with Target 41, sirs," he responded in English, hoping to convince them that he was not in collusion with Marissa. That she was his prisoner.

Marissa sucked in a sharp breath, clearly shocked. *Forgive me,* he prayed silently, not even sure whom he was praying to. Then he stepped aside, allowing the Asazi soldiers access to Marissa.

In the gloom, her face paled, and she spun around as if to run, but they grabbed her arms.

Marissa struggled. "How could you?" Betrayal and surprise inundated her tone.

Finn looked away, unable to face her. Behind the colonel, Kal's eyes had a look that made Finn nervous.

"Proceed." The commanding officer, Colonel Parn, waved them all toward the compound entrance.

Finn fell behind Marissa and her captors, who still held her.

"She's not unconscious." The colonel's voice carried disappointment and reprimand.

Finn paused. "A portion of the additive spilled, sir. I had to subdue her."

"What are you saying?" Marissa's voice was shrill. "Speak English, damn you."

"Where is your vehicle?" Still speaking Asazi, the colonel turned to face him, eyes sharp over his eagle-beak nose.

Finn responded in English. "It died. I had to carry her."

Marissa turned to face him. "How could—" Her voice was raised, a scream almost.

One of the soldiers clamped his hand over her mouth. "Silence."

Kal stepped closer to Finn. Too close, Finn noted. Placed his hand on Finn's, pushing it...

Confused, Finn looked down. Kal's weapon holster was unsnapped. Kal wasn't usually careless. Finn looked his cousin in the eye, but couldn't interpret his expression.

"Halt." Colonel Parn raised a hand, halting the procession.

"Lieutenant Ramont, you were ordered to come in. You've been insubordinate at the very least."

"Sir—"

"You will stand trial. You could have risked our mission. And you brought her here, like this—conscious. You know the regulations about witnesses. We made that clear in the briefing. The Asazi cannot afford being exposed to humans."

Finn feared that his color would broadcast his emotions. Maybe even broadcast his plans, his thoughts.

He seized Kal's weapon, grabbed the colonel, and gestured for the soldiers to back away. "Leave the woman."

The soldiers looked at the colonel, then at the gun. Colonel Parn nodded. "Go. Leave us."

Marissa poised to sprint, leg cocked.

Finn looked at Kal. "Don't let her go."

Kal took Marissa by the hand. She jerked her hand back and forth. Getting behind her, Kal clamped his hand over her mouth, sealing her protests in.

"Don't hurt her, cousin," Finn cautioned in English. "Colonel, I don't want to have to kill you. I need Merck's vehicle. And I want a moment with my cousin. In exchange for that, I'll let you live."

Colonel Parn addressed the soldiers, face stern. "Bring Merck's vehicle to the edge of the thicket. Leave the keys in the console. Tell Merck to wait in the compound. Tell the general I'll handle this situation, at any cost."

The soldiers double-timed away.

"Finn." Kal started to speak but yanked his hand off Marissa's mouth, a bite mark that had drawn blood evident. "Curses, she's a hellion." He swiveled her to face him, then addressed her in English as well. "If you do that again, I'll be forced to give you something to make you unconscious. That's your final warning."

Marissa's open mouth closed, green fire blasting fury from her eyes.

With Marissa now subdued and silent, Kal turned to Finn once more, this time speaking only in English. "We can trust Parn. He's one of us."

Finn studied Kal's face, looking for an explanation. "Us? What us? What are you talking about? There's no us."

"There's an 'us' you don't know about," Colonel Parn interjected. "A group of us is working, fully sanctioned, but deep undercover, to determine a better way to assimilate, to reach our final passage to Earth."

"Finn—" Kal began.

Finn had had enough. "What the curses. Kal, you're a part of this? This—whatever this is?"

"Yes, and my father, and yours was too. We were hoping you would join. Spearhead the movement, even."

Finn looked to his commanding officer. Colonel Parn nodded.

"Who knows of this?"

"Very few at home, and only the two of us on this mission." Kal said. "Now three, counting you."

"Four," Marissa whispered.

"Give me a moment, Colonel, Kal." Finn took a step closer to Marissa. "You know I wasn't going to let them take you in, right? You know I'd—"

He didn't want to say he'd have flown off; a part of him still didn't want that secret shared. Not yet. He had trusted Kal all his life, but what if there was some sort of chicanery afoot? What if Kal was being used to gain information or manipulate Finn? He searched for the right words to explain to Marissa that he would have died before he let harm come to her. He wanted her to know, even if telling her would wreak havoc on him if Colonel Parn and Kal were lying.

A part of him didn't want to believe that Kal was lying.

"Marissa." He put his hands on her arms and pulled her close, until their faces were almost touching, his lips almost on hers.

She looked back at him with eyes aglow, partially with suspicion, it seemed; the other half... He couldn't pin that emotion down.

CHAPTER 37

"I would have died before I'd have let them take you." Finn's face was sincere, his color a greenish-blue in the moonlight.

She knew deep down that this man was honorable. And she did think of him as a man. He was more man than many men she'd met on Earth. She knew he'd have died for her. The problem was, she didn't know why. There was so much to process. So much confused her. And now these two new men, Colonel Parn and Kal, who evidently was Finn's cousin, might be offering some sort of salvation. They'd all reverted to English once the two soldiers had left.

She rose up on her toes and put her lips close to his ear. "What is it that they're asking of you?" She breathed him in. His scent and warmth were a comfort, even on a night that wasn't cold.

"We're going to find out right now." Finn stepped back, but put his arm around her shoulders, drawing her close to his side. He addressed both men. "Please use English. I don't want her alarmed any more than she already has been."

"This is 41?" the colonel asked Kal.

Finn put his hand up. "She's not 41. Not anymore. Her name is Marissa. And I won't harbor any secrets from her."

"Let's go for a ride," Kal suggested. "It will lend us better privacy."

Though the four of them started toward the car, Marissa was concerned. In a car, Finn wouldn't be able to fly, so he'd have no means of escape. She eyed the gun in his hand, idle, pointing down, and hoped he'd at least keep that.

The colonel drove, Kal sat next to him in the front seat, and to Marissa's relief she and Finn took the back.

Seated behind Kal, she couldn't help but notice that the man Finn called cousin looked just like Finn. He could be Finn's brother, his twin, even. She looked from one good-looking Asazi man to the other. Yes, they definitely could pass for twins, at least in this lighting. Same profile, same military haircut. Finn was a little larger, like he'd done more physical work, but it wasn't substantial.

A few moments later, the colonel began to speak. "Years ago, after your grandmother joined our community, a plan was formed. The Asazi have several factions: those who want to stay on Kormia, those who want to migrate as a whole and attempt to overtake areas of Earth, and then the last group, ours. We wanted to begin our passage to Earth in a different manner, slowly building up property, means, and opportunities to start fresh, without building suspicion. It's not impossible. Compounds exist in countries where there are no records, no reliable data. In many countries, in different ways."

He continued, "We have a compound that we are ready to disguise as a right-wing conservative group that is in favor of less government. We have a monastery in Greece that hasn't received any attention. An orphanage in Lebanon. Several military compounds in the Middle East. The list is not endless, but it's extensive."

Marissa wished he'd get to the point. All this talk meant next to nothing to her.

"What do you need from me, specifically?" Evidently Finn wasn't interested in a long explanation, either.

Kal turned to face them. "You would be the first to start this. To prepare an area for us to bring a few over. Migrate several of those of us who want to start over, subtly and peacefully."

"How do you propose to do that?" Marissa couldn't help but ask, even though she knew she had nothing to do with it, and if Finn weren't here, she would have been killed as a witness.

"Leave Finn here. Set him up on one of the properties we have and prepare for a small influx of relocators, every so often, as we can get them over," Kal explained.

"It won't be easy. Our governing body doesn't support this effort. The greatest support lies with the first two factions, not with ours," Colonel Parn added.

"But either way, that means Finn can stay here? And not be in danger?" She couldn't help the flood of joy and relief that swept through her, even though she had no reason to think that Finn would be a part of her life.

"Not in danger from us. We'll have to create a convincing story. But if he's discovered by your kind, he'll be taken in for observation. He'll be a prisoner. A lab animal. And if the wrong people discover this on our end..."

Marissa knew that could mean a lot of things. She didn't want to think of those things. She looked at Finn, whose gaze was focused on the road, his expression unfathomable. Maybe what she should be doing was figuring out a way to get out of here. Alive.

"While you guys sort out your plans, do you mind taking me home?"

Finn's head snapped in her direction. His expression was still unreadable.

CHAPTER 38

"She doesn't know how you feel about her?" Kal asked Finn in Asazi.

"I suppose not. How do you know how I feel about her?" he responded in Asazi.

"Hey. Not fair." Marissa grabbed his arm. "English."

Finn reverted back to English. "Sorry." He took her hand. "We were making plans about returning you. I don't think you'd be safe. You're still a target." He turned to the colonel. "Unless we tell them she's dead."

"Yes, but she can't go back to her old life, even so. Someone will know, sooner or later. Our researchers will find out. One day. Somehow. They found her through her medical records. They flagged her chromosomes. It will happen again if she ever has a medical procedure done. If she ever has blood drawn at a lab. It will go to the main database, which the Asazi have access to."

Marissa bit her lip, chewed on it. "Great. Just great. So now I'll be wanted, but by an alien entity? By some group of aliens who want me? I can't even tell my legal authorities about it. Who would believe me? That's not very reassuring."

"I have a thought," Finn said. "She can go with me. She'd be safe. From the Asazi, anyway."

"Wait a second." Marissa rubbed her temples, stress written on her face. "I'm in the middle of a battle to keep my restaurant. I'm trying to get a loan, and now you say that I'm going to have to go away? To run somewhere? To hide?"

"You would need a new identity," Kal said. "Something that wouldn't arouse suspicion or the attention of our Surveillance Team." He turned back to Finn. "You didn't say if you wanted to stay. You don't have to. You can go back with us, be the soldier you want to be. The one you've always wanted to be."

Finn glanced at Marissa. Soldiering seemed so very secondary now, compared to the emotions he felt for her. Yes, emotions. He would not deny that part of himself any longer. He would not deny himself.

"You're out of the Binding with Alithera. So what's the problem with the life? You want to be a soldier, you want to be in the action. We're going back tomorrow, and that's what you can be. That's exactly what you can do."

"What's a Binding? Who is Alithera?" Marissa asked.

Finn didn't answer her; instead, he addressed Kal. "You wouldn't understand. You never could."

"Because I don't have human blood, I won't understand? You think that's what's driving what you're feeling? Don't you think that maybe it's something different? Do you give me no credit?" Kal seemed angry. His Asazi skin flickered orange. Definitely angry.

"Why? Because you're older? I should give you credit for knowledge of what I'm feeling because you are older? By one paltry year?"

"Not exactly that, but yes, in a way. I'm old enough to have been in the military longer than you. To have felt and seen the effects of some things."

Fury scoured Finn's nerves. "Don't speak in riddles. Explain."

"I can't explain."

Finn could tell something was going on with his cousin. "What you mean is that you won't."

"Fine, I won't. Not now. Maybe never. But I'm willing to help you."

"Help me what?"

"To help you not return to Kormia. To stay on Earth."

"What about Marissa? They will come back for her."

"Yes, one day they will. In another Wave, when there is one scheduled, if they think she's alive."

"Is there one?"

"Next year."

"I won't have her in danger."

"I can make sure she's taken off the roster." Kal switched back to Asazi. "Will you be Bound to her?"

"I don't know. It's early. I don't know how she feels."

"One warning. Do not let her get pregnant. Human women die giving birth to Asazi babies. Your mother did, and every other one before her. That is why the methodology changed."

Marissa harrumphed, clearly agitated by their decision to stick with Asazi language. But there was no way Finn wanted her to hear this.

"I'll make sure."

"If she does, the only thing that can save her is what they call a Caesarean section birth. But the problem with that is, once the baby is out, they will see the Asazi skin, the Asazi wings. And you will be exposed. You will find yourselves locked in laboratories that the public doesn't know about, all three of you. And you will be test subjects for their scientists."

"It seems you know what you're talking about."

"Trust me, I do."

There was a sadness in Kal's tone that made Finn wonder, but not enough to ask. "I'll make sure she doesn't become pregnant. Tell me something. Why these women? How are they selecting them?"

"Our scientists track the women who have a certain genetic makeup. I'm not sure what they look for. If I had to guess, I'd say they are closest to Asazi traits. Maybe they're descendants of the early Asazi? When we come in for a Wave, we try to get to the area that has the greatest concentration. This time, Houston was it. The next Wave will go to the second largest concentration for harvesting."

"Where is that?"

"Right now that is Tucson, Arizona. They were such a close second to Houston that it was a tough call. There were only two more in Houston than in Tucson."

Feeling safer in the knowledge that Marissa wouldn't put together the depth of the feelings he had for her, so she wouldn't feel obligated to stay with him, he switched to English. "So the next time you arrive, you'll set up a bunker near Tucson? Perhaps I will try to arrange to be near, so I can see you."

"That could prove foolhardy." The colonel finally spoke.

"Give us a moment alone, please," Kal requested.

CHAPTER 39

The colonel stopped the car at a parking spot, and let Finn and Marissa out to have a moment alone. She didn't understand why Finn didn't want her to know what he and Kal had been saying, but she respected his privacy, though it frustrated the hell out of her. She respected it because she knew she was safe, that he wasn't planning anything that would hurt her.

"Kal looks just like you. You could pass for twins."

"Yes, we have been told we favor each other."

"He looks sad. Like he's..." Marissa struggled with the words.

"He may be. But he'll be okay. The question is, what are we going to do?"

"We?"

"You don't think I'd leave you, do you?"

"No, but are you staying on Earth?"

"I think it's for the best. What about your father's dream? The restaurant?"

"I think my father's dream would be to see me happy. And you make me happy. Now I have to find a job, though."

"Kal and the faction have made arrangements. You don't have to work. But we do have to be careful. One, they will still want to harvest you. And two, we can't have children."

Marissa had never given much thought to the idea of getting pregnant. Sure, she'd figured one day she'd find the right guy, and do the two-point-five-kids thing. But now it sounded like that wasn't possible. Probably because of Finn being Asazi. That he couldn't get her pregnant. She didn't want him to feel bad about that.

"I'm okay with that," she reassured him.

CHAPTER 40

Three days later they pulled into the parking lot of a hotel near Tucson, Arizona. Finn had decided that the best course of action would be to pick the Asazi-owned property that was closest to the next harvesting. That way he could see his cousin again.

"So what are you going to do about Kal?" Marisa asked.

I'll see him when they come back."

"More harvesting?" She drew in a deep breath.

He knew she was against that, and that there'd be arguments to come over it. He didn't believe in it himself anymore. He wasn't sure he ever had. "Yes, that's why they're coming. But I also have a way to leave him a message, on a website. He can contact me through that if he needs to."

"And you're a hundred percent sure you don't want to return home?"

"There's no reason to."

He kissed her. He *was* home, as far as he was concerned.

KEEP READING for an excerpt from the next book in the series!

HIS HUMAN HELLION

A wickedly sexy sci-fi new adult serial that continues with His Human Hellion, that brings us Finn and Marissa. A sexy alien and the human hellion he couldn't resist, even when she was his intended target. Now she's someone else's target and he's a planet away. Can he get there in time to save her and the baby she's carrying?

Emotions wreak havoc on an Asazi soldier when he discovers the human he loves is pregnant with the child that could kill her.

Finn has a new mission. Save Marissa. Any way he can. That's no easy task when Marissa is the most stubborn, headstrong woman--correction--human he's ever met.

A spitfire Texan finds herself in love with a man who isn't supposed to have emotions, and isn't even a man, except, he's more man than any man she's ever met before. And now she's pregnant with his child. A child that could kill her.

Marissa jumped out of the frying pan and into the fire when she fell in love with Finn. Now he says the only way to save her life is to take her to his planet? I don't think so.

This book is intended for mature readers. 18+

Elle Thorne Newsletter

If you can't click, just put this in your browser: http://www.ellethorne.com/news.html

CHAPTER 1

Finn's phone vibrated a message. He pulled it out of his pocket, expecting to see an *I love you* text from Marissa. Instead, he found a whole different kind of message.

Marissa: *I'm pregnant.*

Finn dropped the phone as if it were a live rattlesnake. Rattlesnakes were something he'd become accustomed to in the last few weeks in Arizona on the land the Asazi used as one of their settling areas. The compound was remote and isolated. Snakes were the nearest thing Finn and Marissa had for company. Snakes, rabbits, coyotes, birds of prey, scorpions.

He picked up the phone and pocketed it. He'd been walking the perimeter of the fencing, making sure it was secure, and that there was no chance they'd aroused any suspicions or curiosity among the local humans. He scanned the horizon for witnesses. There was no time to waste and running would take longer. He lifted off, using the powerful Asazi wings which had only gotten stronger since he'd discovered them a few weeks ago. He'd become convinced of one thing: that it wasn't Earth food that gave him the ability to fly; it was probably the absence of Asazi food. He wondered what could be in it, and wanted to ask Kal, but also did not believe that Kal would know the answer. Kal would not hide this from him. He was certain of that. They'd always been closer than brothers. Kal would not keep secrets from him.

Like you don't keep them from him? The voice of doubt cast aspersions on his relationship with Kal. He shoved those thoughts aside and brought his mind to his current problem. A much more pressing one. Hopefully Marissa was wrong. Very wrong.

It couldn't be. There was no way she was pregnant. He'd been careful. He'd had her be careful. They'd taken all the precautions necessary for humans not to become pregnant.

He flew at a furious pace, his heart pounding in his chest. When the ranch house they lived in came into view he scanned the yard for Marissa. Nothing. The pickup was parked in the driveway. He landed with a thud, anxious to see if it was true. To see if she was pregnant.

To make sure she was alive.

Kal's words resonated in his mind, reverberating in his heart. *One warning. Do not let her get pregnant. Human women die giving birth to Asazi babies. Your mother did, and every other one before her.*

Now Finn had failed. She was pregnant, and she would die giving birth to their child. A child he'd tried to prevent. When could this have happened?

Something crossed his mind. If she miscarried the child, before it became large enough to kill her, then she would live. His love would live.

He sprinted across the yard, slammed through the door, and ran through the house to find her. He burst into the kitchen.

Marissa dropped the pan she was holding, and it clattered to the ground. "What the hell! You scared me." She focused on him, eyes scanning his face, surveying, taking measure. "Finn, what's wrong? Why are you out of breath?"

CHAPTER 2

Finn had run into the room, a film of sweat glistening on his skin, refracting its purplish-blue color, the tiny scales shifting and glimmering. Considering her news, it was odd for him to be that color. The color of worry and sadness. His face was a mask of concern. She would have thought he'd be happy, overjoyed.

He paused, leaning against the doorjamb, almost seeming to need the support, his chest heaving with every breath.

She studied his sexiness, still stunned that this man was a part of her life. His eyes glowed in the afternoon sunlight, catching the rays, his face sporting a few days' beard. She warmed at the memory of what that scruff had done to the tender flesh between her legs this morning.

She approached him and slipped her hand inside his shirt, ran her fingertips along his pecs, then down into the waistband of his pants. He sucked a breath in, his shaft instantly responding to her touch, firming with the same hardness he'd had earlier that morning when they'd made love.

Behind him, his wings flared, opening with a whoosh of air and sound. They were longer than he was tall, magnificently diaphanous, but oh-so-very-male on his muscled body.

"It's hot outside. You've worked up a sweat." Marissa unbuttoned and unzipped his pants in one smooth move. She knelt next to him, inhaling his scent, all man, all sweat.

She rose and grabbed his hand. As she led him to the shower, she imagined lathering and pleasuring him under the water spray.

She was yanked back by his unmoving stance. His body was a statue, his arm outstretched, his hand still in hers, a frown creasing his forehead. What was wrong with him? He'd never given their sexual play a second thought before. She tugged his fingers. "Come on. Join me in the shower."

Next in the *Ultimate Passage* Series:

His Human Hellion

A sexy sci-fi new adult series that continues with His Human Hellion, that brings us Finn and Marissa. A sexy alien and the human hellion he couldn't resist, even when she was his intended target. Now she's someone else's target and he's a planet away. Can he get there in time to save her and the baby she's carrying?

Emotions wreak havoc on an Asazi soldier when he discovers the human he loves is pregnant with the child that could kill her.

Finn has a new mission. Save Marissa. Any way he can. That's no easy task when Marissa is the most stubborn, headstrong woman--correction--human he's ever met.

A spitfire Texan finds herself in love with a man who isn't supposed to have emotions, and isn't even a man, except, he's more man than any man she's ever met before. And now she's pregnant with his child. A child that could kill her.

Marissa jumped out of the frying pan and into the fire when she fell in love with Finn. Now he says the only way to save her life is to take her to his planet? I don't think so.

SHIFTERS FOREVER SERIES

Are you ready for it?

I have a whole world full of shifters to share with you.

I'm listing them here, in the suggested reading order, though I've tried to make it so that you can pick up anywhere in the series as we all have probably done that at one point or another.

Many of these are organized in box sets for savings. Be sure to visit www.ellethorne.com to see which box sets are out!

Where's the best place to start? Well, probably with SHIFTERS FOREVER.

SHIFTERS FOREVER

Grizzly bear shifters and their mates steam up the pages in these swoon-worthy paranormal romances. From trespassers with hidden agendas to curvaceous women who are ready to take a chance, the stories in this collection will capture your heart.

- PROTECTION
- SEDUCTION
- PERSUASION
- INVITATION
- TEMPTATION
- ATTRACTION

~

ALWAYS AFTER DARK

A spinoff with the white tiger from Shifters Forever: Vax, born Vittorio Tiero. He's the one that helped Kane out during a shifter battle. Follow the Tiero family, a group of white tiger shifters, as they head to America to find love... and heart-stopping danger. Full of romance, suspense, and gritty drama, this red-hot collection is sure to entertain!

- CONTROVERSY
- TERRITORY
- ADVERSARY
- SANCTUARY

NEVER AFTER DARK

Another spinoff that takes place in Europe. Here we visit cities along the Mediterranean and meet the old school Tiero white tiger shifters who are resistant to change.

- FORBIDDEN
- FORSAKEN
- FORGOTTEN
- FOREPLAY

ONLY AFTER DARK

Taking place in New Orleans, the Arceneaux shifters, led by Lézare, Vax's white tiger cousin—on his mother's side—are sure to capture your hearts. The Arceneaux are the black sheep of the family. Lézare doesn't cave to public opinion. He dictates policy in the area he rules and he shuns old school European rules and regimes.

- DESIRABLE
- INSATIABLE
- COMBUSTIBLE
- UNDENIABLE
- INEVITABLE
- INESCAPABLE

BITTER FALLS FOREVER

This romance features Mae Forester's nephew Dane Forester, a freewheeling, sexy, successful, movie star who uses every role and every woman to escape and forget the heartbreak he left in Bitter Falls.

- Unbound

BARELY AFTER DARK

This series features more of Mae Forester's nephews! Grizzly bear shifters steam up the pages in these swoon-worthy paranormal romances. From trespassers with hidden agendas to curvaceous women who are ready to take a chance, the stories in this collection will capture your heart.

- Cross
- Lance
- Judge

Ever After Dark

Get ready to be introduced to the white tigers you learned to love in Always After Dark, Never After Dark, and Only After Dark. See their heritage. Visit

Giovanni Tiero and his brothers Federico and Tito. Get reacquainted with Isabel Tiero and meet her sister Capriana Valenti.

- STONEBOUND
- FORMIDABLE

SHIFTERS FOREVER AFTER

This series follows a group of polar bears in New York. Russian and rumored to be mobbed up, they are a powerhouse of shifters, determining the fate of many on the East Coast. Mikhail Romanoff, Layla's father, runs this outfit with an iron fist. Layla's sexy cousin Malachi features prominently in this series.

- COMPLICATION
- FASCINATION
- MOTIVATION
- CAPTIVATION
- FLIRTATION
- INFATUATION

FOREVER AFTER DARK

A series which takes place in Denver, Colorado. Enter a world of secrets and forbidden love. Panther shifters who who share their worlds with elementals must decide who they can trust—and who they can't live without.

- Notorious
- Scandalous
- Delicious
- Perilous

SHIFTERS FOREVER MORE Grizzly bear shifters, dragon shifters, sorceresses, elementals, and all types of other paranormal beings and their mates steam up the pages as the Bear Canyon Valley clan sorts through trespassers with hidden agenda, hidden military compounds, top secret experiments and curvaceous women who are ready to take a chance. The romances in this collection will capture your heart and leave your head spinning!

- Confusion
- Decision
- Possession
- Illusion
- Passion
- Impression

FINALLY AFTER DARK

Follow a pack of dire wolves as they encounter Valkyrie and Berserkers and determine the origins of their kind throughout the ages, while discovering their fated mates.

- ORIGINS
- CHALLENGE
- DAMAGE
- RAVAGE
- MORE TO FOLLOW!

I do hope you'll be able to join me on this wonderful journey with our Shifters Forever Worlds Shifters and their mates!

To receive exclusive updates from Elle Thorne and to be the first to get your hands on the next release, please sign up for her mailing list.

Elle Thorne Newsletter

If you can't click, just put this in your browser: http://www.ellethorne.com/contact

MY PERSONAL GUARANTEE:
THIS WILL ONLY BE USED TO ANNOUNCE NEW RELEASES AND SPECIALS. AND TO GIVE MY WONDERFUL SPECIAL READERS A LITTLE GIFT.

SHIFTERS REALMS

I have another new world of shifters! How exciting! I can't wait to share them with you!

Be sure to visit www.ellethorne.com to see which ones are out!

Where's the best place to start? Here we go!

IRON FLATS

Wolf shifters and their mates steam up the pages in these paranormal romances. From rovers with hidden agendas to women who are ready to take a chance, to unknown the stories in this collection will capture your heart.

- IRON FLATS EXILE
- IRON FLATS JUSTICE
- IRON FLATS REBEL
- IRON FLATS MAVERICK

MORE TO FOLLOW!

I do hope you'll be able to join me on this wonderful journey with our Shifters Forever Worlds Shifters and their mates!

To receive exclusive updates from Elle Thorne and to be the first to get your hands on the next release, please sign up for her mailing list.

Elle Thorne Newsletter

If you can't click, just put this in your browser: http://www.ellethorne.com/contact

MY PERSONAL GUARANTEE:

THIS WILL ONLY BE USED TO ANNOUNCE NEW RELEASES AND SPECIALS. AND TO GIVE MY WONDERFUL SPECIAL READERS A LITTLE GIFT.

Shifters Forever Worlds

Shifter Realms

For sales and news, sign up for the newsletter! Thank you for purchasing and downloading my book. Words can't express what it means to me. If you enjoyed this read, please remember to take a second to leave a review. I'd love to know what your favorite parts were.

The fun isn't about to stop. Make sure you sign up for the link to the newsletter.

Hearing from you means the world to me. This would not be possible without you and your love for reading.

With much gratitude, I thank you!

It took Elle Thorne years to stop being a closet romantic.

Originally from Europe, she wouldn't dream of living anywhere else but Texas. Unless it was another southern—translation: warm!—state. A southern European by birth, she wants to be near the water and the Mediterranean temperatures if possible.

Where does she like to hang out? Near a lake, a beach, preferably with a latte—extra shot of espresso, please! She's inspired by the everyday men who make dreams come true. She loves a roughneck, especially one with a callous or two on his hands. A man who knows how to fix a car, please a woman, and protect what's his.

Nothing less will do.

ELLE'S NEWSLETTER

To receive exclusive updates from Elle Thorne and to be the first to get your hands on the next release, please sign up for her mailing list.
Put this in your browser:
www.ellethorne.com/contact

My personal guarantee:
This will only be used to announce new releases and specials. And to give my wonderful special readers a little gift.